KEYS IN THE RIVER:

*

New and Collected Stories

Tendai Rinos Mwanaka

Mwanaka Media and Publishing Pvt Ltd,
Chitungwiza Zimbabwe

*

Creativity, Wisdom and Beauty

Publisher:

Mmap

Mwanaka Media and Publishing Pvt Ltd

24 Svosve Road, Zengeza 1

Chitungwiza Zimbabwe

mwanaka@yahoo.com

https//mwanakamediaandpublishing.weebly.com

Distributed in and outside N. America by African Books Collective

orders@africanbookscollective.com

www.africanbookscollective.com

ISBN: 978-0-7974-9551-7

EAN: 9780797495517

© Tendai Rinos Mwanaka 2018

DISCLAIMER

All views expressed in this publication are those of the author and do not necessarily reflect the views of *Mmap*.

Acknowledgements

Tears Runs Dry-Sunset, And She Said "Yes", Ruins, Mangoyi- The Cat, Let Her Go, I Am Now Bullet-Proof, The Black Goat, Thus Far; No Further, Hearts Are Victors, Tears Run Dry-Sunrise, or versions of these in this collection have originally been published in *Keys in the River; Notes from a Modern Chimurenga,* in 2012, released in the United States by Honolulu based, Savant Books and Publications, and the rest of the stories, *A Silly Story Hey, In Father Ganyiwa's Hell, She Is A Witch, Makhebha, The Things That Make Us Human,* are new stories and have never before been published anywhere

Table of Contents

INTRODUCTION

There are, KEYS IN THE RIVER. "Life is one long river a pretty voice sings."

It was after I had read a poem from Cypriot poet, *Nora Nadjarian,* entitled *Obdachloser (Off The Coast, Spring 2009),* and her use of this expression, KEYS IN THE RIVER in that poem, that I thought I could use it as well as the connecting title to my collection of short stories, then entitled *Undying Echoes.* What keys are there in the river, and what kind of a river.

The river is our road through life. I have this particular road I have stayed in for over 24 years, on and off but mostly on, Svosve Road, in actual fact its street, in Chitungwiza, Zimbabwe. When I get outside the gate, I sometimes look up or down the road, and see people walking up and down the road, going wherever they will be going. I have done that for all these years, and I am always fascinated by the life that I see in this street, even now after all those troubles we have been through as a people.

The are people still walking in this road, I know there are those who have walked in this road who might be dead, who might be in other worlds, like a long river, that life is. It is this road as a river that I was thinking of as I used this term to define, to encase the stories in this collection, to describe the life of the Zimbabweans, wherever there are now.

As I said the river is a path through a life, and so the keys is the totality of a life in this river of life. It might be the bad things, the good things, things that makes someone angry, things that make someone laugh, sing, dance etc…, that's why in this novel there are a combinations of stories that might make one reading it feel a wide range of emotions, that embraces a life, that tackles the Zimbabwean soul and life.

There are stories that tackles many of the experiences of life growing up in post independence Zimbabwe, early adult coming-of-age stories, love stories in a world in the shadow of the AIDS pandemic; love connect all these stories, is there any other life defining thing like love to human beings. Spirituality! I decided to deal with that spiritual life that we don't really know and understand that well, how to communicate with departed spirits, spirits generally looked upon as devilish, also things like demons, N'angas, ghosts.., that's I have a number of stories that tries to get into that world, to explore it, to layer it open for readers. They are stories I wrote when I was in my early twenties with their sweet sentimentalities and they are a few stories I wrote in my forties grappling with the residues of four decades of living, and these provide balance to the collection. To live is to learn, to live is an act of struggle. But the struggle in this collection unlike the previous one *Keys In The River: Notes from a Modern Chimurenga, 2012,* where the bulk of the stories were first published is on the individual level, not as a country. Thus in this collection I avoided stories that are openly political about Zimbabwe. I want to highlight other issues that make us who we are as a people, that are not openly political but still an act of struggle, of living.

The biggest import of this novel, then, is how each of us, as human beings, go through all these potentially life-changing situations, regardless of our point of origin, on our journey to finding love, freedom, completeness, happiness, satisfaction and our humanity.

SHE IS A WITCH

She is, she is a...witch. She is a witch!
He doesn't even know whether that captured who she was, but calling her a witch sufficed for him. He had been trying to figure her out all along.

How do you mean? Zura- Zurababel is her full name, asks him. Zura is his new girl. Not really new. He can't tell her she looked, *almost like you, babe.* Only light complexioned, lovely- a curvy shaped peach. Tandazo was an artist's impression of petite, the right things, right places, right measures... He is always drawn to these kinds of girls, and he now feels it's an obsession. Anything bigger has always looked less attractive to him.

Zura is thin, frail, talkative and tempestuous. He has been on and off her for years, never staying any longer than she had invited him. It worked fine with both for some time. At one time he had let her go when Tando, that witch girlfriend of his was around in his life. When you have a witch, she won't allow another girl near her prey mate, and until you fix yourself out of her brood- nothing else attracts you. It was always instances when he was between girlfriends that he found his way to Zura, but when he was with Tando, Zura stayed away.

She was unpredictable, sickly, moody, and illusive. Very argumentative- and her way and only her way alone mattered. He finishes capturing Tandazo to Zura

Confident of herself, was she? Zura asks him.

Not really. It was mostly because of lack of confidence. A confident person doesn't always want to have her way.

That's really how he felt!

Am I a confident person, babe? Zura asks him, trying to point him towards complimenting her, as always.

He wants to say, *nopes,* but it's too dismissive, even a little hard. He can't even be wholly truthful with that indictment of her. He feels her illusiveness- that he had felt with Tando, so he couldn't indict her yet. He wants to know it was different, comes from a different source than that of Tando, so he says.

I can always feel some confidence in you, Zura.

How much? He hopes she is not going to ask him that.

She is not overtly smart. Tando wasn't smart that way too but she was a prickle little thing. She wouldn't have let that pass, but Zura lets it pass. She is a bit quiet as she digests this, she has taken it well. When Zura is quiet it means it's okay. She is happy.

Thanks, she says, her face full of light, a dark ivory light for she is a light ashy-clay complexion. She looks like what an African and Indian mixed-blood would look like, only darker. She has the Indians' structure too; frail, petite, waifish... She says there is Indian blood in her, and another moment she is saying white blood. She is proud of her heritage; especially the father's side and not really sure of it, too. Her father is from Mozambique, and her mum is from Zambia, but she rarely talks of her mother's side of the family tree. It is obvious she is a dad's girl. Tando rather was mum's girl. She had a factitious relationship with her father whom she blamed for abandoning her and her siblings after he had divorced her mum. Thus she had stayed with her mum as her mum stayed a bit trying to fight for her husband. She didn't win. She left for her place, leaving Tando with her grandmother, her father's mother to look after her and her siblings. She often talked about this. It was obvious it still bogged her, made her into the kind of girl she was. Who was she?

I am not a big fan of my father, She would say as they hugged together in thick bunches of blankets and sheets. She was very thin, small, skeletally frail, breakable... She wanted more blankets on her to make warm. He was barely breathing, hot and sweating in the same blankets. Most parts of those two nights she slept over, they were estranged, separated by a layer of blankets, not just blankets, thus he couldn't reach her cold fierce beauty and body.

Why don't you figure a way to forgive him? I understand your feelings though but you can't go on like this.

Yes, I have tried. I don't hate him anymore but I still blame him for destroying our lives and abandoning us.

Yah, he said, But you might really need to walk all the way and let it go and start to have a more closer relationship with him. He knew it was the key to unlock her and for her to become better as a partner and lover.

Yah, I will keep on trying.

For Tando those seemed to be questions he could ask, even though he didn't know the answers, but with Zura he wasn't so sure what drove her to be that fickle and unpredictable. He sometimes thought she was a fairy from some world he doesn't know how to get into. It was obvious that she was in love with him. She even says it several times, but she never makes it lasts, always rushing off, always going away, always returning back to go away- into nothingness like stream swirling around the boiling pot. He is tired of trying to keep her to him. So he only takes what she gives, when she gives. Tando wanted to give him a lot that she didn't have, to be more that is less, but had a knack to get into fights with him.

I want you to cook me fish,

Okay, what type of fish do you want me to cook for you, babe?

Any type is fine by me!

It was on the twenty third of December, about 9 in the evening and she was on her way from Botswana where she stayed permanently, working part time jobs, staying with her sister. She was coming for the Christmas break and holidays, and to see him as a lover for the first time. They knew each other, grew up in the same village. He was a bit older than her, in fact way older, 13 years older than her so he knew her mostly as a little girl, struggling when she was a blooming teenager, and was attracted to her back then but he never took the chance to make it, to say the words. Over 10 years later he had proposed to her on the Facebook where they had been friends for years, and she accepted him straight away. He liked it. He considered that as confidence, but now he was not so sure it was confidence that made her make the decision. Maybe it was flashes of smartness on her. For the past 5 or so months they were texting each other on fb and on WhatsApp she seemed confident, answered a lot of his prickle questions well.

He had great expectations waiting for her late into the afternoons of the following day as she came to his place from her other sister's place in Belgravia. She had arrived early in the morning, and texted him she wanted to take a few hours to sleep off the exhaustion of travelling for over 24 hours from Botswana. When she was coming she had texted him again,

I want to eat my fish when I arrive that side, so prepare them and put them on low heat, I need them a bit warmer. And he could only do as she had requested. He couldn't wait any longer. It had been years and years he had seen her in flesh. In his mind, through the texts, he had developed an image of her, filling up the blanks of time in his mind with bits and pieces from those texts, what they had meant to him. Thus most of what he was expecting of her was a paper Tando, one he had built through social text love messages on the digital liquid paper of his cell phone. He went to meet her at the taxi rank, with his paper image of her.

She is small, that's the first thought that hits him as he glimpses her. At first he is not even sure she is the image he has in his mind, but the small of her face's features start expanding, fitting into his paper image of her, connecting in, locking in, settling in. *The nose, yes, that smile yes, yes she is the one who walks to me, yes the one who hugs me- she smells very nice.* He searches the perfume, there is no text that had built how she smells. He can only accept her for he can't unbuilt the real to fit the picture.

He hugs her like he is hugging incense, afraid it might waft into the blue air, faintly there, she is in his arms. Somehow, she stays.

How are you doing, babe?

I am doing fine. It's wonderful that you came, hey. They are on their way to his place, 3 streets off the taxi rank he had met her. They make small talk on the way to his place.

She is small, he can't seem to stop returning to that. Zura was just as small, frail, more so than Tando. Zura talks and Tando is quiet. With Zura it's as if she has words in her mouth always fighting to erupt out like beer on empty stomachs wanting, fighting to erupt out as puke, and like her- always talking words to name her need to constantly want to disappear. He wanted her to root. Zura only talked silly things like a little girl, things to construct the person she thought she was, wanted to be, wished she was, always exaggerating things. Maybe both the exaggerating and talking of who she was, was her way to make up for her smallness, her not being there when she was there. Tando was a fierce woman for her smallness, a bomb, always touching itself around the bomb's safety nook, always threatening to explode.

Where is my fish, Chad?

It's coming babe, but I want my kiss first. It's the joke they would have all those times they would text each other that the first day they would meet they would greet each other with a long deep kiss, frenching it off! But both were ashamed of kissing at the taxi rank where they met in broad daylight, now he knew he would get his paper kiss. She blushes red and he is galvanised as he abandons the sofa he is sitting on for the one she is sitting on, which is a two seat. She slides over, she is melting into his arms as he kisses her.

It's like being kissed by a witch. This is the moment he starts thinking of her as a witch of some sort. It's a hot kiss, their mouths are hot but he doesn't feel like he is kissing the way he has felt with other woman before her when he was kissing them. He doesn't feel his heart kissing her, or maybe it was her who was not there in the kiss. They mess around for some time before he brings her the fish.

No Chad, it's not the fish I want!

But you said any fish is fine.

Nope, I said I wanted breams.

I don't remember you saying anything specific, so I bought you my favourite, mackerel.

But it's what I would have in Botswana. I wanted something local, something I don't usually have, like breams.

You didn't say that Tando. *Do mackerels come from hell,* He asked himself.

I told you I wanted breams. I can't have mackerel.

Do they make you ill?

Nope, I eat them a lot of times in Bots, so I am not having them now.

But, I had cooked all these for you. Do you want me to throw them away?

Nope, keep them. You can eat them until you finish them, and the sadza as well.

He didn't want to argue with her, so he cooled down as he returned the plates with the food to the stove, and asked her

So what would you have? Matter of fact.

Mmmm… I will let you know when I want something. She says that as she settles into the sofa besides him. He holds her in his arms as they talk and messes, small talk, small messing, trying to probe each other, both physically and emotionally.

With Zura it was music they talked of. She liked music, she was a musician who didn't know what to do about her passion of wanting to be a musician. She did a bit of Music College and dropped. She joined a group and two. She stopped that to rewrite her O levels, which she sat for several times. She didn't write them the last time as she left for Zambia for a year, only for her to return back, into his world again. She was that kind of music that plays but never really plays. She was more sound that music, illusive, gipsy.

I love rock music, I inherited that from my father, she says

They are listening to classic rock music, sitting on the same sofa that Tando would sit in a few months' time. The thing with rock music is it gives these ideas that you are madly in love with the person who you are listening with and connecting with at that rock's level; banal, beautiful, timeless. So the music gets them closer, not just emotionally but physically. The movement to the other happens, you don't even know who moved, who didn't; you are locked in a kiss before you know how to question anything. He kisses her hard, the next room they are people he stays with, but he doesn't even close the door as he kisses Zura. They stop when they couldn't breathe anymore. Abruptly, she tells him she is late on a date with her friend. So, he let her go.

A year later, after Tando, Zura is back in his home again. She has come for a sleep over. Sleepovers have always been fascinating since the two nights Tando slept at his place. It approaches acting like a married person when you are not. You want to act the husband you are sure you can never be. Maybe he wanted her to collect the eggs her twin had left behind, to unlock him. She looks frailer than he had known her, she has been ill. He doesn't know what really the problem with her is. Years ago she confided in him that she had a BP problem. She says she was ill most of the time she stayed in Zambia, that she has constant pains at her sides. She was almost mistakenly operated by the doctors. But today she says she is fine so he is thinking finally she has come to make love to him the whole night, which she had stopped short of doing a year before. He is not sure about her, so at first he is ambivalent. They have the whole place as he was not letting out any of the rooms. So they talk a bit in the dinning as she eats her yoghurt. She has refused all the other foods he had offered, settling for yoghurt the whole night- settling for sugar demons, milk suns, the sacredness of sweetness, no. He can't live on yoghurt alone!

She is toying with his laptop as she spoons and eat yoghurt, and he is thinking she is playing the music, but she has burrowed deeper, she is on his pics. That's when she met her twin sister, Tando. No, they are not related, but she is her sister anyway, and she is curious about her. She asks him who she is. He tells her Tando, an ex girlfriend.

Where is she?

Bots.

Is she married?

Not yet, I think.

Why didn't you marry her?

This is a question he has always found funny. Are we supposed to marry every person we date?

We were on wrong time, wrong space.

Oh okay. She accepts his evasion.

What's she like?

She is a witch…

That interests her. She has always been a bit on the queer. She then tells him she is now practising to be a N'anga. This hits him badly. Why is he always attracted to these creatures? *Am I bewitched, demoniac, cursed…*

Tando refused to sleep with him no matter how much harder he tried to convince her. No matter how much they made love, she would say no when he asks her. He striped her down to her Eve form but she still said no. He touched her woman, the outside, but she refused his finger to enter her, so he spend that whole night, in fact two nights hitting her shores like the oceanic waters but the land refused him to land. All that he really wanted was to make love to her but she refused him.

It was a long way to this from the dinning sofa they were sitting after she refused the fish. Later he had eaten a bit of the fish and sadza; she still refused to eat, refused any food. She says she is full. And at 9 when all the shops were closed she says.

I am so hungry I can't sleep on the empty stomach. I want ice cream.

But all the shops are closed that have good fridges to store this food item.

I need food, or else I am leaving for my sister's home. She throws an ultimatum that is in her familiar territory of doing things, tantrum*atically*. She is the queen of the Ultimatantrum land!

Okay, let's go out and check if we can get anything at the truck shop.

I don't need anything; I need Vanilla flavoured ice-cream.

She wanted Vanilla flavoured ice cream- the first blossoming pollinated by the bees and hummingbirds we no longer name.

Let's go then!

You can go. I will wait for you here.

They are using a candle, as electricity is out, under rationing, the endless rationing that has become his country. It's a normal for him, but it's not for her.

Okay, he says as he leaves her for the shops.

Only to be called back before he finishes closing the door,

Chad, wait for me. I can't stay alone in this dark. In darkness, sense and sound had become unfamiliar and powerful, and it entered her.

He could only shrug his shoulders and wait for her. They go to the shops in the thicks of the dark. The whole place is in darkness. Two streets over the familiar dog barks his pidgin. Telling him to wait, be patient, all things come in time. They get to the taxi rank where there is a tuck-shop he wants to check for food. Then her ice cream is replaced by roasted corn, Demeter of grain, holy, stripped. So she asks him to buy one corn cob being roasted for sale by woman hawkers at the taxi rank. He buys two in case she starts pestering him again in the middle of the night with her hunger pains. They get home and prepare for bed.

He is playing her beautiful music, Enya's music from the album, *Paint the sky with stars*. She loves this music, its new music to her. She asks him to leave the candle on and the music playing. It's a candlelight thing. They get into bed straight off. He is hungry for her wetlands, but she plays him slowly like the song *If I Could Be Where You Are*, playing on his speakers. It's him who added that song to this album for it wasn't part of it. He tucked off her blouse and unhooked the bra to reveal his favourite land and he is confronted by her girls. One girl's eye is closed, broken, removed; it's just a healed wound. He caresses that one first. It gives him the feeling he has whenever he hears the song, *Memory of Trees*. He doesn't know why. It is his favourite Enya track; it invokes the feeling of not having the thing that was important to you but only the memory of it- missing it all the more but still living without it. Even when he feels a little revulsion and swarming pain as if he is going through the pain she had to go through- the pain of loss- he is still not sure of not touching this girl. Maybe it's a subconscious feeling: a protective feeling, a victim's feeling, a fight against the normally strong humans' god-insect feeling of favouritism. Maybe it's because he knows she would instantly know he was a little bothered. Is he really bothered? When he is bothered he starts talking amid making love, but he can't seem to talk, he is the quietness in the song *Watermark*. So he licks only one eye and that eye gives him direction like the song *Evening Falls*, on how to caress the wound where the other eye should have been. He is a brave soul, he knows he has entered unchartered territory. Though he had met a girl who had a small mop between her breast before- and it had prepared him, maybe to understand the body is never perfect, but this was a totally big thing. She had lumps, some big, all over her body too. He is afraid one of these will be talking cancer. Or maybe another person inside; there has to be someone inside her who would deform her in that repulsive way.

That night all that he could do was to familiarise himself with her body. She says *no* every time he asks to enter her. So he gives up early on, and sleeps off, as a light December misty *Celtic Rain* showers above the asbestos roof, and moves him into the plucking erosive clanging music and feeling in the call part of the song *Lothlorien*. And the answer part is a deeply soothing reply. In his psyche Tando is the call part, Zura should have been the answer part, yet Tando's twin had a different story why she couldn't sleep with him. She said she was preparing to enter her calling of being a N'anga so she was afraid of pissing the spirits on her by making love to a man.

So why did you come if you knew very well I wanted to make love to you and you also knew you had things in you that do not allow you that.

I just wanted to spend the night with you, and make you see how much I am ill and what you will be dealing with the rest of your life if we are going to marry.

We are marrying now, really!

But I keep quiet a bit, and she prompts

Are you comfortable with this?

What!

The possibility that we might never consummate our love.

You can't ask that of me. Why don't you like sex?

If I have sex I get terribly ill. I have done that before I know it; I get locked and become stone-frozen in pain. I am afraid this time it might even kill me.

Really! He can't believe this.

If you love me you have to accept this, also you have to enter the same calling with me, supporting me.

He chuckles off the rising anger silently as he says,

How can I go back to a world I left over 20 years ago?

They had stopped doing traditional stuff in his family- over 20 years ago, and were now all Christians. He knew the futility of that world. He doesn't believe it anymore.

So what do you want us to do?

I don't know, He answers her.

You have to commit now.

You can't ask that of me. He sticks and stops there! If he had answered her yes more than no at this point he would now be boasting of that like a woman who has lived her life as if it were-music only to discover it was lawyer*ing*.

12

She slides off his stomach where she had been making love to him, not making love really, maybe where she had been ministering her call. He didn't even get to remove her panties. She raged when he tried and told him the things on her would fight him. All that he could make do with were her tiny boobies, which in a few minutes she said were irritated and painful. He is hard but he can't even come. He asks her to blow him, she does that a bit with her hands but still he can't come. Then she says she is tired and her hands aches, and thus she had started asking him to commit. To what! To a few cat scratchings all his life, no ways!

He takes his side of the bed and sleep. In the morning, he is bored with her. He is cross with her. But he is polite; he buys her eggs and bread, whilst she cleans herself. The smell of confectionary things, cinnamon of boiling coffee, once upon a time, was the breath of god, falling from phoenix nest- heavens of humans- to bless, restores his lost soul a bit. And when he tells her food is ready she says thanks, but she doesn't like bread and eggs. She says she should be on her way too. She had shoved a cream cable-knit sweater, put on blue jeans, fur-lined suede boots and triple down coat- cold in disappointment.

He gave her taxi fare, and accompanies her to the taxis. He hugs her goodbye. He knew he wasn't going to stick around. The same day he was leaving for South Africa.

He is angry, mostly with himself. He is also angry with himself the following morning after their first night with Tando. She didn't leave in the morning like her twin. They settle in the dining room after breakfast, still fooling around here and there, but he knew he wasn't going to get some. The collision of sounds as the afternoon began its fadings, the neighbours growing annoyed, him frustrated and angry pushed him to tell her to leave and that he would look around for another girl who wanted to take it all the way. She starts crying, he feels guilty, so he apologises for his cruelty and callousness. She accuses him for wanting only physical pleasure with her. Which she seems to be for, except the sex, but he comforts her and tells her he loves her. He really does love her. They start talking deep stuff about her family, her growing up. Finally, he gathers courage and asks her,

What happened to your booby?

I developed mumps that were so bad they ate into the nipple. I was treated for the mumps eventually but it was too late as my grandma didn't have enough money to take me to the hospital in time. So when I was treated the nipple had been destroyed and it has been just what you saw.

You don't have cancer?

No, the doctor said I don't have. Those are just lumps.

Okay.

You are fine with that? She is trying to build a story; an entire story of their relationship around her deformity by the process of elimination, not creation- only negation.

Yes, why not?

There is this boyfriend I dated a few years ago…

She doesn't tell him the name but he knows the guy. They are distant relatives with this guy so he knew about the relationship from their shared connections.

When we made love for the first time he was repulsed by my body, and said very hurtful things to me and it still hurts.

What did he say?

He said I had a demon man in me and it's that thing that deformed me and so he couldn't be with me.

Oh! He could only say that. *Didn't I think of the same thing last night?*

14

He dropped me, just like that. He put on his clothes and left. I haven't spoken to him since.

Halting words, still heavy with pain!

I am sorry.

It's okay.

She is vulnerable and breakable. He likes this her more, he falls for this her. He doesn't like the fierce her. This her is not the demanding bitch she was yester night. The fierce her barked half-backed truths at him like that next street dog, especially when they were fighting, it would aid her with its half-backed tirades. He ended up working his fight with her around this her. When it was in the room, he found himself becoming circumspect, silent, accepting, watching what he said. He chose his words carefully around her and when she wasn't there he could ask her anything. He didn't care to lose the fights. But he still didn't know if it's this deformation that mangled her psyche or it was everything.

She leaves for the rural homes they grew up in some moons before, and a week later she is back in Harare. She sleeps off at his place again. This is her last night in Zimbabwe before she leaves the next night for Botswana.

They do everything, everything as long as he doesn't get to her woman. At one time he thinks he is going to enter her, but she changes her mind as he reaches her precious mouth, and wriggles off. She looks for her pant and put it on. It's futile, so he stops. In the morning this repeats again. It's a yes and a fat no. He is exhausted, but he tries to be polite in the morning. Deep down he is desperate, so he asks her to stay with him but she is not sure. She asks him to pay her parents lobola. He says he is not yet prepared for that. She says she has her things in Botswana. She wants to go back to sort her stuff and she will return back to stay with him, in a few months.

He knows the truth; there is nothing for her to stay for. A broken sink, cardboard doors broken onto two cardboard kitchenettes, broken sofas, dirty coffee table, old mattress torn into several holes by the rats, old four plate stove on the far banks of his kitchen, dusty floors, promises, expectations, hopes- he only senses their absent eyes after she is gone, the feeling each of them generated in him- lost. He later tried to call her from Botswana, to relearn their helpless, hopeless alphabet, vowels, consonants, but it's impossible to hold onto her. His insides is full of broken things, pilled all over, there is no room. After some time he also discovers he was not really interested in domesticity, except as product design.

Tando leaves him troubled, and now he leaves for South Africa troubled by Zura. He decides, maybe they were all three too much the same, copies that could become original again if paired with other personalities; he hides his leaving in this writing. He builds his surroundings on absences unrecognised, empty spaces, which kept him sane and helped him to concentrate on himself. He notices Zura's absence by 2 months, but by then too much had already been subtracted from Zero, another loss meant nothing.

He thinks there is something wrong with him that attracts dangerous and damaged people to him. He has to learn to know this specie from far away, a specie that seemed to be after his soul without getting involved in the mining. So he drinks a beaker-full of the old south through a cubist period where he visualises about her from memory, her various parts connected by chain words, forgotten spaces in the narrative, until he could write about her as he wanted her to be, as broken and disconnected as she had made him feel. Until he couldn't see both Tando and Zura walking barefoot over his heart, until they begin to feel clumsy, like Gulliver, too big, too confined, too hot outside, yet too cold inside.

If they were to return with empty suitcases, then he will embrace them like a halo held by a halo, but if they were to return back with full suitcases, he won't embrace them, he will kiss the past, one lip touching the other, an anxious hello held by a hello. If they were to return back into his life, he would demand to see that their lives had gone through a full panel beating before he could accept them back. It is not even 2 months later, since he started staying in South Africa, when he met another of these species. It was like meeting yourself all over again, but now he was strong enough to see his face from far away.

She says she is an atheist, but she is fascinated by traditional spirits, and she thinks she is a queen witch. She doesn't want to marry and have kids. She is frail, stubborn, and difficult- and pretty it hurts! She has a blood complication problem. She, like Tando and Zura, has psychologically wounds he doesn't want to deal out his soul to again, so he shuts her out before she damages him more. He is a stone at the bottom of a woman-built lake, a stone that grew gills and learned to live in the deep dark bottom he build for himself, until he grew fins and swarm back up to the surface, gulping for air, destined to be one who walks on the land. And on top of this water, he doesn't believe in any spirit world anymore.

This is his safety net!

TEARS RUN DRY: SUNSET

No one has ever had the right to tell me what to do. Rather than a right which can be demanded, the act of listening to the guidance offered to us in our challenging moments is a privilege, a recognizing of value, an admission of connection. There was a time I could have listened to what other people said, but that time was long over. On that quiet night, I walked, feeling nothing, not even a connection to my own self. I simply and silently placed one foot in front of the other along the path of pure pain. Half clear and half an echo, the conflict between my love for Monica and my self-loathing agreed on only one thing: the destination.

As I moved to the Speciformis tree -we called it the Mususu tree- to the east of our homesteads, I felt satisfied with the road that I had chosen to walk, though it was such a committed path. Perhaps for the first time, I knew the truth: the suffering on this road of life is benign and impermanent. I also wanted to think that this is how my friend, Misheck, felt so many summers ago as he made his way along this same path, as he made the decision that I now faced. It was the middle of the night and silent; I could almost hear the sounds of the Mususu tree as it is rustling, heaving and murmuring excuses.

Maybe, it wanted to be excused from participating in the night's imminent calling; or maybe, it's swoosh-swoosh whispers were prayers for me? No one was awake to witness me, in my booze-befuddled way, as I approached the Mususu tree. It loomed there in the darkness. I wanted it to enclose me in its many tree limbs and boxed-arm branches, to embrace my weary spirit, and to assure me of my new direction. With each step I made towards this tree, shadows shifted, causing a deceitful play between light and darkness.

I thought about trying a different way, but I was not so sure that the promises beckoning were the right promises for me. Fear wisped away any resolve to what little light was left there in the shadow of the Mususu tree. With a cold and mysterious power, the dark and irresistible shadows returned me from my indecisive moments and sped me headlong into the branches of the tree. What would then come of these light-sowed frontiers which had flitted for a brief moment before me?

Should I have prayed? Did I ask for forgiveness? Was I worth forgiveness? Should I have asked to be accepted to the eternal place? Was that mine too? But, who could accept me? Not me, not my kind, not the faint-hearted, haunted, has-been who desired to become part-of? Shortly, I had the rope that I had carried tied securely to a big strong branch with a beautiful loop that would fit snugly around my neck. In another moment, I was high in the tree, the loop around my throat. The abyss yawned like black dye from below; deep and attractive, it drew me into its dark embrace. And, I let it pull me in.

My hands grabbed the noose at my throat to loosen it as I bounced at the edge of the shadow. I felt my hands grappling for the rope. My hands were sweaty and slippery. I tried to heave myself to a branch above to release the chocking that had engulfed me. Part of me said that I am not going to die, but another part told me that I was surely already dead.

I couldn't breathe; there were yellow sparks all over me, which turned to orange, purple, and then a dark violet. But, before passing out, I moved down memory lane, re-living life over again. Visions of my past came as surging waves on the ocean's beach, as did the pain which centered, converging from all over my body. It was like being punctured by tiny painful pins, wounded by hundreds of thousands of these little pins thrusting into my inner body. Pulsing, these pins ascended to a zenith in mid-air before descending slowly into my flesh. The pain subsided and the visions drifted in again.

There, I was in my second year at the University of Zimbabwe. Playing soccer, my friends and I were in the second half of our game when a member of the opposing team intercepted the ball from my team-mate. I ran out to recapture the ball which had gone near the neighboring volleyball court. Someone there picked it up; but instead of throwing it, she brought it to me. We met one another's eyes and I, diving deeper and deeper into her eyes, never seemed to reach the bottom. There was magical pheromonic attraction broadcasting on all frequencies. I felt us settling into the warmth between us. I could have kissed her straight away.

This closeness was broken when my teammate called after me for the ball. What my strike partner wasn't aware of was this starry imperative which had taken hold of me. Nevertheless, I threw the ball to my friend with all the force expressive of the anger I felt at having been disturbed. My face: a damaged constellation!

When I turned back to her, she smiled and I thought -If I could just be the answer to such a sweet smile. Then, she strode off in a lolling beautiful gait, innocently displaying the full curvaceous quality of her body. I remained glued in my place, eyes reaching out for the specter which now lingered there with me.

I played the soccer game with my friends until the end, but I wasn't into it anymore. My wild eyes had turned inside. My soccer opponent might as well have simply walked by. And, by the end of the game, the fields had become backlit by a low falling sun. Searching around the grounds for her, excitement built at the edges while I fell in love.

Yet, she was nowhere to be found. I searched around for her at the campus, but failed to locate her for the next three weeks. How do I describe those three weeks: with which words? I know it sounds silly, as if I was nothing more than a little boy.

What moments of agony!

Three weeks later, our accounting class was hosting a lecture on financial management for the marketing students. It was to be three hours spent peeling the onion of knowledge. However, what mattered most at that moment, though, was the absence of her smile, which seemed to have been absorbed by the atmosphere around me. It was not a true silence, what was in me, but some kind of solitude. The guy who usually occupied the desk to my right side had left for the day. I hoped that whoever was to occupy it wouldn't be distracting. Lost, I hadn't even cared enough to look around during the class.

When given the opportunity to ask questions at the lecture's end, I heard the guest acknowledging someone whose voice floated to me as if from deep memory, a voice like a song, a polyphonic epiphany, a wind-stirred Lorelei. I turned to see who owned such a beauty of a voice. I didn't want to lose track of my muse again.

When she finished her question, she darted a glance at me and I knew it was her. At the end of the lecture, I was the first to stand up and purposely stride to the back row. I caught up with her as she exchanged pleasantries with one of my classmates. He was probably making sketches, preparing for a future go at her, but I cared enough to not give him the chance. Oblivious to his protestations, I burgled into their conversation by greeting her and ignoring him. She agreed to meet me later that afternoon.

That was the start of the whirlwind twisting through ragged mountains, through the dense thick forests, through the wild raging seas, through memories of rooms that I never left, through memories of rooms of invisible walls, through memories of rooms that I had existed in, but never lived inside. In the midst of all the madness, I found a love that I never thought existed.

I was born the only child in our family. I had never gotten to know my father for he had left my mother when she got pregnant. When I was born, she had tried to look around for him so that he could take some responsibility for me, but he was said to have left for Botswana.

My mother never heard anything more about him. So, she raised me with the help of my grandmother. Later, she married a new man, but I didn't go to live with them. I stayed with grandmother in the rural areas of Seke. I had a half brother and a step brother from her marriage, but I never got to know them well because they stayed in Harare with my mother and my step father.

Later, the family, everyone except my mother, died in a car accident. In the face of this tragedy, my mother returned home to my grandmother and me out in the country. Sadly, my grandmother died a couple of years after Momma returned to stay with us. Our life, there, was quiet. That it is to say, it was quiet until the day I came home ready to say the thing which had weighed so heavily on me.

"Momma, I have something very important to tell you."

That's how I started the conversation. She was surprised, stopped knitting, and was attentive to whatever I meant to tell her. Every part of her body was focused on that moment.

"You look pretty serious. What could be the cause of this mood, Tate?"

"I went to see my doctor."

"What? Are you ill?"

I didn't know what to say, but I still remembered the doctor's words as he told me of my condition. He had assured me that I was not ill, not that I believed him.

Should I have said, "Momma, I have this kind of a condition"?

Or, should I have told her that I was simply ill? After all, that condition led to another. And, therefore, in the long run, I would be ill, so why differentiate between them when the whole thing meant that I was ill?

"Yes...I am ill, Momma."

"Ill? But, from what, Tate?"

From a wound inside me which will never stop paining me!

Are all wounds supposed to heal?

Are all wounds supposed to be painful?

But, I don't know any answers; I only know of shadows. I remember only sparks exploding, wishes for the choking pain on my throat to stop, and for my legs to stop dancing on the air.

My mother was busy exploring my head with her seeking eyes and hands. Then, she moved to my face, especially my eyes. She felt for my heartbeat, touching my forehead, hands, and throat. After a few minutes and in a rather assured voice, she asked me again what ailed me. I also remembered Momma's doctor saying that we could save Momma from a premature death by hiding devastating disclosures, that thinking a lot could cause her blood pressure to soar and hasten another stroke which may do her in.

Since then, it had always been my duty to hide disclosures that I thought could be detrimental to her health. After all, it was still my duty, even as I tried to avoid her searching gaze. Was she really strong enough to receive this bomb? Yet, I had to take the risk for she must have grown somewhat immune. Here I was, for the first time, staring into the ghostly eyes of death.

I must die and how soon no one knew except myself and who then could have known the cause if I hadn't told those that I loved. I had no guts to tell Monica so it had better be Momma; I only hoped that, with the disclosure, I wouldn't do her much harm.

"Momma, I have been diagnosed HIV positive."

It took mother a good five minutes before she could say anything in reply to what I had said. In between, I almost panicked. She had remained quiet and static, but her gaze revealed the depth with which that disclosure had sunk. I also could see that, deep down her eye's sockets were brimming with tears.

"Oh no, no, no, my boy, I am so sorry."

She said that and embraced me in her reassuring arms and we remained locked in each other's embrace until I felt the wetting of my shoulder back. I knew she was crying silently. Tears being the last thing that I wanted to give vent to again, I told her to stop because I couldn't take anymore of anyone's crying.

After an effort, she stopped and started asking me about this and that, the "why's" and "when's" and, in a good hour, she was herself.

"That doesn't spell anything for you; I am sure your doctor told you so."

"Even you and the good old doctor know, like the hot-hell, it spells death, my dear Mother."

"Not for a long time anyway," she concurred.

"But, in-between I have a life to live, huh?"

"Yes."

She agreed, readily.

"But, I will still die and, so, what's it worth anyway? I mean this life you are talking of, when you know that one's own life precariously hangs in the balance of death's jaws. Tell me: what life could that be Momma?"

I know that one day I shall wake up extremely ill, that I will be a burden to everyone, an emotional stress, living my life empty of love because I couldn't be able to give it out without hurting somebody, without killing. I would be untouchable, like a leper. I can marry, but it would be absurd and ridiculous.

She shook her head and clucked her tongue. She knew that my heart was breaking.

"Tell me, Momma, how could I live this life knowing that I destroyed someone's life with my stupid follies?"

Then, like someone drowning, but lucky to have a chance to draw-in a fresh breath of air, I stopped and took a heavy breath of air. I continued in a spent and subdued voice.

"Tell me: what life could that be, Momma?"

"Tatenda, listen to me, son."

She took me with her arms and fiercely stared into my eyes while some alchemical reaction turned her speech into pure silver and golden nuggets of motivation.

"We are born to die one day or another, whether we like it or not, Tate. There's only one thing for sure; death is a dark thing without footsteps. It comes with no warning. As we live and enjoy our life without an ailment to worry about, we fail to realize that our existence is all too fleeting. Those who have this disease think to themselves that they are dying just because they have the disease and that the disease kills, yet they should be the ones with the ability to be sure of themselves and have the foresight to come to terms with their lives. They are already aware of their situation and what it ultimately leads to. They should appreciate life, realizing its fragility."

She continued, "Tate, there is no excuse when your time is up. All of us, to the moment of death: we are warm and urgent, unaware of the empty spaces waiting to be filled by memory's photo negatives, the moments we will leave behind. You are blessed, Tate, because God is saying he is not yet ready to take your life. God is saying: 'My son, take this life, live it fully, because you deserve it'."

My beautiful mother stopped to catch her breath. She knew the importance of her words and rose to the occasion. "I have always thought you were a fighter, Tate. What's gotten into you? What is it that has made you so lazy as to succumb to such a minor snag like this? What is it, Tate? I know your fear, baby. But don't give in to it. There is always someone hurt in the process. Don't ever forget that, Tate. Don't look at this with anger. Smother that which is gaining ground in you with hope, determination, and the belief that you can succeed, my son."

It must have been her best speech ever because it helped me to get some courage to look at the whole predicament with a fresh pair of eyes. Sadly, there was still an inside joke. In my joys, I had savored life's beautiful and tragic truths and time had come for me to fold my arms and welcome this sweet, sweet, truth: I was now weary of life; I no longer felt as if I belonged anymore to this insecure world, a world so insecure that I was being punished and sacrificing someone for doing a thing only once when others whored on a daily basis, but lived.

Maybe there is such a thing as realizing that your life is doomed. I had discovered that about Misheck. We were in the sixth grade and were friends, but he always had problems, existential problems... Misheck came from a very poor family. His father neglected them, abused them; the father was a drunk, a wreck. His mother tried her best to take care of them and protect them, but often failed. One morning, I awakened to hear that Misheck had tried to commit suicide by poisoning himself with pesticides, but had survived. Afterwards, I had difficulty connecting with him. My mother was concerned for my safety. She said I should stop playing with him. Anyway, after a couple of months, we played together again. Deep down, though, I was still afraid of him. He was cursed. Anyone who tries to kill himself is viewed as cursed. It was thought that nobody should play with him, talk to him, or talk about him. Had he succeeded in killing himself, nobody would have cried for him. There would be no funeral for him; surely, he was going to hell.

By the time I went to bed, it appeared to Momma as if I had accepted her advice. That's what I wanted her to sleep on that night. For the first time in years, I came to a conviction that Misheck had been right, that killing oneself was a better option sometimes. Talking with Momma that evening had galvanized the immediacy of suicide in me all the more.

Momma also asked me, during our moment together that evening, whether I had told Monica about my illness. I lied to her, saying that I was going to tell her the next day. I said all that to tap into and drain my mother's anxiety over me, but I knew that such an opportunity was never going to be. Telling Monica about my illness could have given another name to it, hope, not HIV. I didn't want to embrace this name; hope means to be positive. Giving it this name, hope, had consequences. Because of hope, I would have to be positive about a situation that was hopeless.

And, so, I briefly found myself amidst my mirthless dance there, at the end of a beautiful branch of the Mususu tree. Languid now, the dance slowed; pain drifted away again and memories wafted into my mind, riding in on the last molecules of oxygen.

The memories started from the day when Monica and I spent our first night together. The next day, we went out for a walk and a movie. Then, we returned to my place and spent another night together. That night, I looked into the seismology of our love, inside of which was measured the softest rumble of things. Apart from our minds making dreams, our bodies had also created mythologies beyond orgasm, in our touch, our feel. My body and mind in synchrony had connected to my innermost intentions. It was on that night, our first to make love, during which I came to a fateful decision.

I went to see my doctor. I gave some blood samples and was told to return for the results the coming Friday. I told no one that I had been seeing the doctor. The week of waiting was one of the hardest and longest in my life. It seemed the minute hand of the clock had gone on an eternity's leave and, like the stupid thing that it was, the hour hand had followed behind. After what appeared an epoch of waiting, that Friday arrived.

Had I reached the end or was it the beginning? Did I deserve some choices, did I merit hope? Even though I had been straight and faithful to Monica, this did not, could not make up for my experience before I met her, could it? Wasn't Misheck deserving of a second chance in life, too? Misheck had told me he was leaving school after the end of our form two classes. He left to go to a farm that was nearby in order to work as a general hand. He wanted to earn some money to get by and help feed the family. Maybe, he thought he could leave behind all his problems. It didn't work. The next time he made the same fateful decision, and this time with resolve, he succeeded; he slipped into eternal unconscious with the help of a handful of painkillers.

On Thursday night, I slept at our rural home at Mayambara. My appointment with the doctor was the next day at ten. I was there a good hour early anxiously awaiting the doctor. I couldn't eat or sleep; my whole being was curved around this appointment and what the doctor would say.

After what appeared just a couple of minutes, I was summoned to the doctor's office. Was the race really over? Finally, with jelly legs and a funny tip-tilting stomach as if I had been drinking sewage water, I made it to the doctor's office. While the good old doctor scrutinized the papers as if he couldn't believe what was written, I uneasily waited for my verdict. After a few minutes of silence, I asked him in a broken voice whether I had the disease.

The doctor started to say something: then, stopped. He tried to look into my eyes, but failed to meet my questioning gaze. I knew I had AIDS. I was struck by the fear that touches a fish in the pond when it is covered by the shadow of the fisherman. I just withdrew inside myself.

He came behind me and held me by my shoulders and said..
"Yes."

Even though I knew I might have the disease all along. I always tried to assure myself that maybe I hadn't caught it. It was that hope that had given me enough courage to find out the truth. Now, faced with the truth, it was hard to process. Why hadn't the test turned out the other way?

Why had I hoped for better?

"You don't have AIDS, but you have the virus. You are HIV positive, Tate." The doctor spoke reassuringly trying to make me feel that there is a difference.

"With a positive condition, you can live many years. It's what you make out of this life that is important. You should start living positively, eating healthier food, being hopeful, and involving yourself in exercise and sporting activities; shy away from alcohol and drugs. I also think you should call upon the advice of counseling agencies for they can be really so much help to you."

"I prefer to keep to myself."

Surprisingly, my voice had returned. It was so steady as if nothing mattered to me.

"You can only destroy yourself by keeping to yourself. I think you need to tell your parents and, above all, Tate: you also should tell your girlfriend and get her tested as well, if you have one. Then, you can see what you can plan for your future together."

Suddenly, it hit me. Have I passed the virus to Monica? Is she going to die because of me?

In that instant, I knew which road to take. I knew I could never ever recover from what I was feeling. I knew the time had come for me to do what I had obsessed about for a long time. I knew painkillers would be an easier way to die, but it was hanging that I deserved. It was the only thing that could wash away the pain I was feeling and pay for the wrong that I caused Monica. I wept for Monica and for the predicament that had befallen her by loving me.

It took the doctor nearly half an hour to calm me down. He must have given me a lot of advice; in my anguish, though, nothing grabbed my attention. I remember nothing.

On my way out, I managed to thank him and assure him that I had no intentions of leaving anyone in the dark, but also knew that I could never pluck enough courage to face Monica with that disclosure.

I went to look for her at her lodgings. I knew she was home because I had asked her to wait for me there...

Hanging there from the Mususu tree, I re-lived this conversation with Monica and felt nothing. Emotion had washed away. I only knew the darkness all over me. On the far side of the pain, the ink-black darkness seemed so gorgeous; I relished swimming through it. But, not yet...the memories still beckoned though fainter, more distant.

"Monica, I am so sorry for wasting your time. I have had a change of mind. I need to keep to myself for a long while."

My voice had strength enough to reach her even though it didn't have a sound. It was carried only by darkness, the yawning blackness which had begun to wrap around me when I heard the results of the test. If darkness could have a voice, it was that voice which reached her.

"What are you saying, Tatenda?"

She seemed not to believe her ears. Should I have talked to her about my condition or our condition for that matter?

No, over my dead body, never!

"I can only serve to give you troubles and that's what I have been doing."

"No, you haven't been giving me troubles and you know that yourself, so whatever are you trying to say, Tate?"

"We don't have a future together, Monica."

"No, no, no, wait a moment."

I held up my hand to motion her into silence.

"I know this just like I know the back of my hands. Please don't ask me how I came to know, because there is no answer to that. I am so sorry; we simply don't have a future together, Monica."

"Please stop this, Tatenda. What's gotten into you? Is that the wonderful news you promised me?"

She wailed frightfully as if seeing a hissing snake which was about to strike.

"You have another girl!"

"No! Another girl? No, no, no, it's not that." I shook my head, not believing what I was hearing come from my mouth.

"So, why are you doing this to me, Tate, knowing how much I love you?"

31

"It's not about that. You know I have nothing to complain about you, Monica; don't you know that?"

She nodded her head, but still had lots of queries.

"It has everything to do with me, Monica. I don't know how best I can express it for you to understand..."

"You really have to try Tate because this affects me; I have to know what it is that's eating at you."

"Come off it, Monica!"

I was almost about to tell her, but had to find a way not to.

"I can't help thinking you are still hiding something very important from me, Tate? We have always told one another the truth no matter how much it hurts, Tate. Are you keeping that promise?"

She probed me suspiciously, probably still wondering what the heck was wrong with me.

"Monica...there are some things better left unsaid because it's not wise to say them. There are extremely sensitive issues that are so shameful and painful to say. I want you to find just a very small ounce of forgiveness in your heart and use it for me. Please don't cry."

I felt so rotten to be the cause of her pain. I embraced her and held her in my arms. We started a torrential outpouring of tears together. For awhile, I was absorbed in this state and carried away by guilt and broken promises. Deep down, though, I knew that I had to get away. As the tears started drying and she was able to hear, I bade my farewells.

"Don't ever think that I don't love you. You are the only one that I truly love. It's me who's the problem. Please forgive me, Monica. I hope that someday if we meet again, then you won't still feel I wronged you so much that we could never be friends again, Monica."

"Bye, bye, my love."

I touched her shoulder as I started walking toward the door. I opened the door and turned. Monica was looking at me, her face wet with tears. She begged me to stay. I wanted to stay and comfort her, but I couldn't.

I just couldn't. Darkness neither comforts anyone, nor does it have a voice.

"I wish you the very best that this life will offer you. I have had my share..."

And I had become darkness. It had crawled into me and been given voice through me. My oxygen starved mind seemed to have finally wound down, already a shade, a creature between the dark and light.

And, as the ink swallowed me, I heard someone calling my name: Was it Momma watching me hang from the Mususu tree? Or, was it Misheck welcoming me? Perhaps it was Monica still begging me to stay and see everything through together with her?

I felt only the winter's chill.

THE THINGS THAT MAKE US HUMAN

We were restless; it was the draught year of 1992. We had just completed our "O" levels and we had little to do, and a lot of time on our hands. This combination is dangerous. We were dangerous. We were latchkey teenagers. The days seemed like 36hrs days but they passed off as 12 hours days. When you are hot-wired and restless with a lot of time on your hands- you are hedonistic and young at that, you end up trying crazy stuff; you just get around to that one way or another. You influence each other, and the next moment you into defiance mood and anything can pass.

We had just come from the river where we spent the whole plucking day playing football in last season's river sands and we wouldn't swim in the river's small lakes as it dried, the water was so dirty. We couldn't stay inside homes at night, we decided to walk off the hotness, to have a date with the ghosts of our areas. We were hot as flames so the ghosts; which were hot as flames- were what we wanted to be with. The night outside was beautiful. The red wisps of the willow stood out in the night sky, there were fireflies bopping their lights on and off through the wisp of the wallow. Through the wisp I could see the fireflies and the few stars in the skies, whilst the wallow was swaying through the gentle summer breeze- it was a visual orchestra.

Our area is full of spiritual beings, ghosts, and all that loot that makes you shiver with fear. You grow up inhibited by these so as you get to that defiant age you really want to defy these things because they are the last things we conquer; they are really part of us and resides inside us- in our psyche. They were two of which, the ghosts and the spiritual beings who were the owners of our place. Our area is of Wanyama tribe and totem and growing up they were many rules, too many sacred things we were supposed to abide by and respect, let alone the ghosts. I think one can take that up to a certain age, and then defiance sets in and you start confronting them, and everything else.

*****

This ghost is known by its name, not by its shape, we had heard our adults say, so we had decided to visit this ghost at Parumano cemetery. Its name was Parumano Ghost. We had heard from those who had encountered it that this ghost, a woman of the adjacent village would demand to have sex with you. Hell, we were hot and horny like nuts- we wanted to get laid. Since ghosts were bloodless, we decided to forgo condoms. In our crazy teenager sex starved minds each of us assumed we will impregnate it. We had been told the sex was great with this ghost. This woman had been married and the husband had killed her whilst having sex with her, with pleasure of-course! She had died having sex with her husband, so in life beyond the grave she craved for sex and would have it with anyone she felt she wanted who would pass through the road besides the cemetery. As we upped our way from Gowa RekwaMatimba valley we started calling for it as we head toward the Parumano cemetery.

Come out bitch and meet us, my cousin, Daniel, called out.

We want to fuck the hell out of you bitch, says my cousin's friend, Andrew.

Today we will impregnate you, I also called out.

We kept shouting for it, invoking it to rise from the beyond and come for a fuck. We were nutty crazy as we hollered in the middle of the fields where no one could hear us. The sounds of our voices got disappearing shadows, and they replied back, *are you my husband*. We tried to look for the sounds of our words but we saw wide faces with lines that resembled cracks in mud. Hair gossamer blackish bluish reddish brushed backwards, frontwards, sideways like a windstorm reckoning that started shaping on this face.

I looked at her; I tried to focus on her: it was like staring into Augusts' dust storms, the one that was said to be transport for the spirit mediums of our areas as they travelled from one part of the area to another, but it was night, thus it gave the impression of electric blackness bloating out the sky. The wind hurled rust-coloured leaves through the air, the arthritic branches of trees swayed rhythmically. Dust bloomed lolling above her eyes like a mystic halo. Her eyes were the hardest substance known by man. She thought they were pretty

Her hands dancing at her sides, arms straight as steel, fingers loose as hair, I try to touch a flailing arm, to cool her. My hand dissolved into her hand, I reach out to pluck my hand and it too dissolved into her, not as liquid but into her being. She started absorbing me in, as I try with brute force to stick to where I was standing, feet firmly planted down, in a tag of war poise. My companions tried to steady me by holding me by my waist but we couldn't fight the force and strength of this women, as we entered her, all of us, not just our penis. We entered her woman as full humans.

We encountered buried villages from long ago, the names of which we couldn't read. The language had died millions of years ago. Yet we knew it was a language portent with life from far off memory. In these villages we could make out spiritual beings busy making love to each other. No one was doing anything else. We became transfixed, watching this human endeavor being practiced in a far away world to us. It was like an open brothel and we were the spectators. No one bothered about us; it was like we were not even there! Can lovemaking beyond death go on without a single snag- I had doubted this, for nobody had followed it to know for sure. It seems time had stopped in this place to shield itself from itself.

There were broken building nailed to the mountainsides, of dagga and wood, broken bones, broken words, more broken words without meaning, fingernails touching, so much hair all over, flaps of dried skins, the smells, and then we see our Parumano ghost coming to us from the other side as a dark talking cloud reclining upon the mountaintop. It was her shadows instead, they said, *are you my husband*

We said, No, we are not!

So why did you want to sleep with me? Ugly tenor sax voice, wine lip, clamped sinuses, dragon's breath, sparrow's nest in her mouth, and a brain tripped tongue.

We are just naught boys, we thought we could have a little fun, I said.

Are you having fun now? She winked her eye which climbed all the way to the heavens and covered half the sky with long eye lashes.

No, please let us go, my cousin's friend, Andrew, whined with fear, a fear that smells like an old town abandoned.

She laughed; it felt like clanging cymbals playing in a far off cave, as her eyelashes came down to settle on her face. Despite the absence of an inspired wind, all fallen leaves around us laughed with her too, busy reporting to their invisible God. Her mouth was liquid red fire, and when she talks or laughs, flames blew out as little fireflies we had seen on the willow tree.

That's what naughtiness becomes of you!

We are sorry!!! We beg feverishly, We are sorry!!! We are sorry!!!

Don't be sorry, you have entered me, so you have entered the spiritual world of ghosts. I can't release you until you have made a date with the ghosts you wanted to see tonight. She smiles, a smile vast and white, a little kind, a little detached, like the milk-creamy ceiling of a room where you have woken up migraines.

It was not a very busy road as it was way out of the villages into the fields so they were not a lot of men she could choose from, nothing had to be wasted now! No one was there to hear us, too.

*****

We were four of us who had left home for this excursion, me, my two cousins, Amon and Daniel and a cousin's friend, Andrew. I lied to my mother that I was going to my cousin's place, and when I got there, we lied to my cousins' parents that we were going to my place, and then we went to Andrew's place, when we got there we lied to his parents we were returning back to the cousin's place. In the middle of the way home, at the willow tree, that's when we diverted and took the small road to Parumano cemetery, which was beyond our homes and fields, between our village and the next one.

Now, we were scared shit but adrenalin was pumping through us galvanizing our nerves as Parumano makes us her captives and transports us deep and deeper into the ghouls' world. We were enmeshed into this moment, we were now the moment.

*****

Ghosts were said to be afraid of too many people and so we thought if we were to stick together we would get our bitch and get laid. We had thought if we gang rape the bitch it would make our

38

place habitable again as she carried the babies quietly in the grave. We were tired of living inside our hearts, always afraid of these ghosts and spirits.

We were now confronted with a world we had no idea to empty out of. We were her bitch as we were carried in her electric blackness to the south. All the blackness pulled in, animated, fierce and beating like a heart. We each had two hearts, the ones still inside our bodies and the ones outside, in this electric blackness.

We had intended to visit all the troublesome ghosts of our area, and as we bedded inside the Parumano Ghost, it took us to the Lion Ghost of the Nyadirika gulley that had been changing into the lion, which is the spirit medium of our area. Surely standing waiting for us at where the gulley really channels into the earth, off the road to Dzimbiti and Nyamukapira villages, we found it. The lion was our own totem, me and my cousins, and the friend was of the crocodile totem and we knew we would protect him from our totem. We knew the lion would never eat us as we will never eat it in our real lives; it was a sacrilegious thing for each to eat the other. Like it was a sacrilegious thing to marry a husband or wife of the same totem with you- so we approached it with fierce determination.

Mhoroi Shumba Nyadirika, we greeted it. It growled menacingly as it flies at us upto our faces and stops shot before attacking us as it growls with fierceness. It shook us to our core.

We knew it wouldn't touch us. Our friend; Andrew's heart was pounding, his eyes were like wild poppies, but he held onto our back. The lion was a mixture of black stripes and brown, eyes; two feral shocking holes, the colours a mirage in the winds of Parumano Ghost.

Why do you terrorise people who passes by here, I asked Nyadirika lion.

This is my land. I am the spirit medium of this area. I do whatever I want. When Sekuru is thirst in this dry galley and becomes dangerous, my people have always known what to do. If you are my people as I smell, it tells you everything, so you shouldn't be asking me this question.

But you are giving bad name to our totem, Gwara, Daniel says, and I placate it and defended ourselves, our ages.

We are only children; we don't know what to do.

We knew what the Nyadirika ghost was saying but it was beyond our purview. We were not the elders of this place. We wouldn't know how to do the appeasement ceremony.

Please stop making life difficult for the people, Andrew deep in our backs stammers, and the lion roars. We held firm and start our totemic offering in a pleading call.

Tine hurombo mhukahuru
Maita shumba gwara sakarombe
Varikuhozi mukarekwa ndiani
Maita Gwara, tiri vana venyu
Mutsikapanotinhira, mudyazvirihwo
Mufambanepanyoro, maita shumba
Gwara sakarombe mukarekwa ndiani

We knew we were not doing it right but we knew it would appease this spirit of ours. We kept on it until it started moving slowly backwards into the galley, slow by slow it faded into the galley, being replaced by the dark electric blackness of Parumano ghost as we started moving in a whirlwind off to the east.

We knew we were taking off to Mariga bus stop, this is where Parumano ghost was taking us. Mariga Ghost is the one that accompanied those who disembarked from the bus at night. It's a white clothed ghost; you would see it off a bit of distances, walking off from the bus stop into the gardens area, sometimes into

Mapfurira village. So a lot of people had been duped into thinking it's a fellow human being and would call out, *hey, please wait for me so we would walk together,* and then we heard Mariga Ghost answering Parumano Ghost back,

Run, walk faster, catch up with me.

Thinking it was talking to us.

Handisini ndakakuuraya iwe muroyi, (I am not the one who killed you, witch) Parumano ghost replied it from Amon's mouth.

The white thing stopped and looked back at us tensed for attack.

What did you say?

We said we are not the ones who killed you in a witch fire, Parumano ghost repeated through my mouth.

How do you know about that? You are little kids, so who told you about my life. Still thinking it was talking to us!

Were you not a witch? Andrew asked it.

I was not a witch, little boy. I was falsely accused and they burned me in a fire over 900 years ago. I once shared ash with the soil; I am now talking to you from the dark yonder theatre, a darkroom. So be careful about the accusations you are making. I have to live in this embodiment for the next hundred years, terrorizing my tormentors through tormenting you people until I do 1000 years of restitution. It's not mine to decide to stop, but each of us has a burden we have to carry, something we would like others to overlook in favour of our essences.

And why did they falsely accuse you of being a witch when you were not? I asked.

Because they were jealous of my gift. I had the gift to see things that were beyond human eye. They knew my gift will undo their witchcraft, so they connived with the kings of this area and had me killed as a witch, when in actual fact they were the witches.

Who are they?

My husband's other wives. We could feel the swarm of anger still inside her as she said that. And then she became vulnerable, the round cheeks sculpted to reveal high chiseled cheek bones beneath eyes framed by a fan of bountiful lashes. She was a beauty in her past life!

Where are they?

They are in you?

In me, I am Parumano ghost, I told her. Dark colours, intricate colours, stained guilty, made from other leftovers colours covers me as Parumano Ghost in me bridled with anger.

Go back to your area bitch, the Mariga ghost thundered as it runs for Parumano Ghost. How can you accuse me of witchcraft, bitch? Were you not killed by a penis?

These two ghosts were the world's mournful noises now looking for payback. Closer, we could see her well as she flies toward us, she was in legs that looked like super pointed slick shoes, she runs- the runs confident, the point of the foot looked like the points of a pick- direct, unencumbered by any dirty earth. We wished the points bended a bit, they might have conversed with each other and garner gumption to tell her to stop walking away off Mariga station and lead people astray.

You witch; I will show you a good lesson,

Parumano Ghost whirled out of us as if it's the sun ordered by a planet, as it dangerously swerved ahead for the white Mariga Ghost. Before they collided the Mariga Ghost blazes into a fire- the elements wind and fire exploded. Dust stirred up them like smoke after a bombing. We could only watch as the dust enclosed us and pushed us into the gardens area. We knew we were now in the brood of a mixture of the Parumano and Mariga Ghost. It was better that doing a goose chase with the Mariga ghost, calling and answering each other into Mapfurira. We still needed to confront the gardens ghost.

And if we were the unsuspecting traveler we would have increased pace trying to catch up with Mariga ghost but couldn't, for a kilometer walk into the heart of our village. It will be a game of calling each other out until at roughly the top of our homes where several roads diverge, one going into the fields, two going to the next village, one going back to Nyatate, and the one from Mariga, and there it would burst into flames. But the flames that busted before us were different; there was necessary burning, there was dark anger. We knew with the burning of the Mariga Ghost many people of our village and the adjacent villages will never be victims to this ghost again.

Not even the queer gardens ghost would be afraid of Mariga Ghost anymore. The gardens ghosts had stayed so quiet in the wake of the Mariga Ghost, since this Mariga Ghost had started using the road that passes through its haunt. This gardens ghost is known as Dhora Rangu Ghost. As we got to the gulley that runs between the gardens, and it is the side gulley to Nyadirika gulley. Whilst Nyadirika flows westerly into Madasanana creek, this gulley, known as Mudondo gulley flows to the east into Nyajezi river, and close to Nyajezi river that's where we met our date, Dhora Rangu Ghost. It would just surprise an unsuspecting traveler at night when it says, low in the sandy soils around the road, *Ndoda dhora rangu*, asking for a dollar from us! The sound of his voice strikes me like a falling apple. Her voice is sandy blue, moody blues, melodic, dripping with emotions- we are not surprised as we very well knew he will ask us for a dollar. He sleeps, gleams in the sands, lying low; skull like old parchment, with two shocking holes mirroring his soft clouded filled brown eyes from the previous life and a clever, lively smile peering out at us. We are wordless amid this ruin. Dwarf-dark undertones spun around us; drugged, castrated, gutted and drowned in cement in one night when he was 16, stories abound that the person had been killed by a local general store dealer to increase flow of customers into his shop which was at Nyatate shopping centre. His pieces were mixed with muti and were buried in the concrete cement of the shop front entry, and these would attract people to enter this shop rather than the other shops at this shopping centre. Another story fragment to substantiate this was on the other parts that I had also heard speaking in this business man's grinding meal. The mill had been running nonstop since morning; they were a number of funerals in our area, after a bus disaster that had killed children of a local school. Thus the miller had to meal maize flour nonstop to be used for cooking of sadza for the people who were at these funerals. Late afternoon, instantly there is someone clapping hands inside the milling machine, then the mill stops, and then a man's voice is heard saying,

Ndizorodzei ndaneta, meaning, *please rest me, I am tired.*

The grinder starts clapping hands, and says,

I am so sorry, I forgot to give you rest, Sekuru.

Then the grinder leaves the mill for the home of the business man where it was said he will give it water to drink, some said blood. The skeletal remains of this Dhora Rangu Ghost were said to be in the residence of this businessman. The grinder was said to pour water or blood on the bones. When it was quenched, he returned back and continued grinding until another unplanned oversight, another day.

But at the gardens, as long as the people asked for a dollar throws one in the sands, afraid of the consequences of noncompliance, the ghost would let them pass. But we had no dollar so we said,

No, we don't have money for you.

I can't see you. Dhora Rangu Ghost complains. Surely he can't see us. We are in a smoke cloud of two fighting ghosts.

Yes, you can't, fucking thief. Tell the one who killed you that we are never be robbed again.

We knew we could intimidate it as we were clothed outside by Parumano Ghost, and hidden inside Mariga Ghost. Dhora Rangu Ghost couldn't touch us. But if we had refused to pay it and were not protected as we now were, it would have enmeshed us in a huge cloud of darkness until the sun rises up. Then we will find ourselves stripped, and a dollar taken out, or just stripped naked-the clothes gone. The dollars it took were said to be the taking of people's wealth and giving it to this businessman. That dollar would always make you want to go and buy in his shop, whether you know you are enmeshed or not. And the businessman got richer. People at night using this road would walk with a dollar, and they would throw this dollar into the sands and the ghost will collect. In the morning people had checked for their dollars, and found-nothing.

After nuetralising this ghost as it peters out into the sands, we now wanted to confront the Bus Ghost which was just across the river Nyajezi, a bit off to the south of Gomorefenzi Mountain, at Chibvuri cemetery, just behind Manjoro residences. It would show up early in the morning to travelers who were rushing off to catch early morning buses to Mutare and Harare, so we returned back to Mariga Station.

You will instantly hear the drone of the engine of a bus, and for minutes what you see is the dust and dimmed lights, just off the graveplace near the road, and then the bus will become visible. If you are a traveler you know you have to run to the station, or else you would have to reschedule your journey as there was only one bus that went as far as Harare, to dance in the capitol steps.

And then we saw it coming down the road from Manjoro home; it stopped to take passengers at Chibvuri bus stop. We knew it was the ghost; it was too early in the morning, around 2am. Then it proceeded into Nyajezi River, off onto Mariga station where we were waiting for it, and it stops to take us,

Harare, Harare, a shadow person calls at us

Yes Harare, we answered as we entered inside it.

Predicate of presence, imagine a dimensionless white galley, and then off it drives to Harare. There are a few people in it but these people don't see us, even though we see them. The shadow person comes through the aisle calling for people to buy tickets, but he can't see us. We are clothed in several ghosts now. When we got to Ziko Mountains and homesteads, off to Nyatate, also finding nothing fits this white gallery, someone, I think it was Amon, started a song; no sound, no words, and our voices rich in longing joined in. The people in the bus can't see us, the ghost can't see us but both hear our music. There is pandemonium as people shouted they were in the ghost bus not the actual bus. There is crying, swearing, but no one sees the door as they are clothed in the darkness of the ghost. We kept singing a song about the life of this ghost, telling her to go back with people where she had picked them. The people joined us when they realized we were not the ghost. We told it these were not the people who had killed it through a bus accident during the liberation war. Thus it should stop changing into a bus and terrorise people. Her voice keeps wafting above our singing like leftover dreams.

This is my house. If you happen to walk in, always know that you and my house are unrelated. You are just a tourist.

And as the droning sound of the bus thinned out into the atmospheres until it is quite completely, I hear the last faint whisper- horse, guttural, hovering under and above all sound like a chorus of toads: *This is my house. If you happen to walk in, always know that you and my house are unrelated. You are just a tourist.* But we were now at Ferro galley. We knew the Bus Ghost had released the people it had taken captive with us back to Chibvuri bus stop and took us north to Ferro galley, and then wafted to Chibvuri cemetery, where that last whisper had come from. But it was near us. We knew we were already in the presence of the Baobab Ghost.

If we had not intervened those few in the bus would have thought they are on their way to Harare, only to discover, a bit later, after waking up from the slumber they were in, that they have been deposited at Chibvuri graveplace. As the sun digest the eastern horizon, coming up from the dawn blue Mozi mountain, it will light their mind, and they will realize the actual bus passed them whilst they were sleeping at the grave place. They will scuttle in a hurry trying to get to the bus station, but it would be futile. They have to reschedule!

*****

And at first the sound is a forced mantra and we both recite it.

This is my house. If you happen to walk in, always know that you and my house are unrelated. You are just a tourist. There is zither music. This is new territory for Baobab Ghost; it had never before made small talk on the way to its manifestation, let alone song. It lamented in pain, oppressed with rusted chains.

They buried me in the baobab tree, It started talking.

Who killed you? I asked it.

The liberators.

Why, Andrew asked it.

They accused me of being a war collaborator, and killed me and threw me into that baobab tree over there. She pointed at the baobab near the Ferro mine.

Even though the baobab has now closed the entrance inside its trunks, my bones are still inside that tree, thus I take the form of the tree to terrorise the unsuspecting travelers at night here.

Why do you haunt this place?

That's where they killed me.

Go back to the baobab and grow with the tree. That's now your home, go back! I admonished it.

Go back!

Go back!

We kept saying that as it left us, filling the deep crevice that remained with corroded waste inside us.

The Baobab Ghost of Ferro Valley, was near Chibvuri gravesite, a bit down from the gravesites in the middle of our road to the graze lands in the resettlement areas. This had been its place of haunt, now it will never come back to this haunt place.

The resettlement areas were the only places that still had grazing grass. There, where you cross the gulley, it would surprise the unsuspecting cattle herders, mostly young boys and girls like us who were coming back with the cattle, a bit deep into evening or night. It would start a very small ring fire, almost a glowworm, then it would start growing branches, growing up, ringed like a baobab, the stem pushing out, branches growing bigger and bigger, the fire staying on top of the tree, until it is a huge massive baobab tree in front of you. You can't run when it starts, your knees get locked, your mouth dries, no word comes out.

It's a weathered experience, time torn, wearing tortured scenes-wishing they were dreams, not the boys' own framed reality. She had eyes like illustrated pages of the mad man's ruminations, one larger than the other. Then it would explode quietly with no noise, as lightening. One of her ears as she exploded were like a mine shaft, the other like a window, large window in a desolate wilderness, hanging there in the skins of the air, like a bed and breakfast room in the unvisited plains. Lightening is always useful to this ghost, lighting like strings, burnt cities, ruins and then she disappears. The sounds of its disappearing were lazier, feebler, the light gone, but the pounding of the boys' hearts. Those across the river waiting for the herders would see that, and know the herdsmen are confronted, and the cattle have run awry, all over the area, so they would cross the river to help the herders round up the cattle after the Baobab Ghost has exploded.

Many cattle might not be found until the following morning and some would stray into the nearby fields to graze the crops, and that's another problem the herders have to deal with afterwards. You will only know that the herders are out of the locked slumber of this baobab tree when right after it explodes you will hear the herders crying out, now freed off the Baobab Ghost's lock.

Go back!

Go back!

Go back!

We kept admonishing it as it died out. It is now two eyes in a hideous head, legs of misshapen fetus, back of a dog, clothes of stripped skin.

She leaves us at Andrew's place on her way to her next brief shelter, next campsite, and next ruin. I feel I am now quicker than these vast selves. Her very absence as we wake up adds something to the solemnity and starkness of the morning. We are only conscious of cymbals of the sun clashing on our skulls. We are sleeping outside the house, looking into the skies bursting with the sun. It was like watching splintering fire flares from a sun we had forgotten existed. There was something sweet melting as I breathed the morning sweet air, little shivers of breeze moving on top of our faces and exposed arms.

AND SHE SAID "YES"

"Hello Lucky!"
I was left dumbfounded, unable to speak a single word. I wanted to say hello and, at the same time, ahhh?

I was so surprised.

It had never occurred to me that she might actually greet me. Isn't it surprising to be acknowledged by someone who always maintained silence whenever I tried to engage her? But, one day, out of the dot-less blue blue sky, she said hello to me. It was the first time and, I hoped, certainly not the last time.

One beautiful summer morning, a Saturday, three years ago, I remember being at our local shops, the Zengeza 2 Shopping Centre with my two best friends, Geoffrey and Patrick, when I laid my eyes upon her, the most beautiful girl in the entire universe. She was coming from the shops oblivious of the young man, trailing and desperate, by her side. Obviously, the young man was trying to entice her, to get her attention, but she appeared as if she was walking alone, leaving him to her silence's torment.

It was quite clear that she was at the height of her powers. Her beauty and posture mesmerized Geoffrey and Patrick. We couldn't help but agree that she was a delightful creature.

I said to them, "You know what? I am going to try all the tricks in the books to talk her into having an affair with me."

I paused and thought a bit to make my next words have the kind of emphasis that I wanted. "Where has she been all of my life and where might I ever find her again?"

"There is no need for you to worry about that; I should think we can trace her whereabouts. After all who would be faulted for tracing such a delightful bird? Take heart, man!"

Such enthusiasm was uncharacteristic from the usually pessimistic Geoffrey.

"She is young, around twenty."

Exploring, ruminating on the intersection of the moment, I wondered if, by simply speaking it out aloud, I could be saying something true.

"Yes." Patrick replied and added, "...but..."

Always true to form, Patrick always puts "buts" in everything.

"For all that I have seen, she wouldn't talk to you, not likely, didn't you see how she was ignoring that young man?"

Yes, yes really, he was somehow correct at that because the girl had ignored that young man as if he was insane to be talking to himself. For all that, I was not discouraged, not even by Patrick's buts and negative reminders.

After all, who would have admitted to himself that he might be rejected? Who, please? Who would have accepted that he doesn't measure up to this and that kind of level? No one.

I mean nothing, absolutely nothing should be considered to be out of our grasp. We often reason against reality, especially if it's not molded into the way we want things to be. We always want to win no matter what, even when the momentum has been tipped against us. That is: inside of us; we think highly of ourselves and no one should try to convince us otherwise.

Surprisingly, we met her again as she returned from wherever she had been. We had been at the shops for the past hour playing mini-soccer and snooker and getting trendy, flashy haircuts. This time, she was moving more gracefully and slowly as if it was more leisurely to walk alone than in a group of people. Such was her truce with time!

When she was but a couple of paces ahead of us and walking towards us, I stopped suddenly and stretched my hand for a handshake. I offered her my greetings behaving by all counts as if we were once blessed with each other's good relationship. This schoolboy trick seemed to work with her because she stopped and offered her hand as if offering it to a relative last seen ages ago. She is wondering who the relative is and whether he has changed over the years...I thought to myself as I started talking.

I don't remember what I talked about; but, after a few words, she perceptibly withdrew inside of herself and left me there struggling to build a foundation for a relationship.

Getting acquainted with a girl sometimes follows the process of building a castle. You want to lay a good foundation by assuring the girl that you don't mean harm and that you want her to be friends with you, and yet, perhaps also more than that. Or, like you are attempting to construct a rainbow bridge, hoping she will see this rainbow bridge and acknowledge your worthwhile efforts. You try to draw her into a free flowing conversation by talking about the weather or about the last harvest or whatever endeavor you have been up to. When you think you have a solid foundation, there emerges the rainbow bridge to your castle; your castle which is supposed to soar high into the air.

On this day, however, my castle was unbalanced, sometimes going this way sometimes that way, going a little higher, a little downwards, a little forward, backwards...I had nothing, a popped bubble instead of a rainbow bridge. This girl started by ignoring me and then, as I tried to paint my bridge and castle, she drew more deeply into her own self. Yet, there I was at her side, talking to her, but looking more like I was carrying on a finely nuanced and textured conversation with the thin air.

Behind all that talking, behind all the words I was saying to her, behind all that fear which had started to grow in my head, my insecurities began to snuff the light that was flickering in my heart. This fear found its way to the deepest part of my heart. Later on, I saw ugly fingers festering all over my heart. Those fingers of fear were sycophantic. They busily dug, looking to tap the warm blood of my circulatory system.

I had tried all that I could; I mean I had tried to draw her into an understanding which proved as elusive as holding mist in my palms. So, I retreated back with an empty handful of hope. I felt cheated out of my life and I didn't know whom to blame for that, other than her silence and the fear that was now in my heart.

Over the next year, whenever I saw her, I always tried to start a conversation, but it became obvious that she was not interested. My friends had even tried all they could to help me, but met the same silence. Yet, when Geoffrey told me to rest it... and from Patrick, to stop altogether, I rejected their advice. I accused them of giving up too early and too easily; after all, there is an old wise saying that says: A faint heart never wins fair lady.

Even if it meant I had to be driven against the prickly barbed wire, I didn't want to give up too early or too easily. After all, it's the fighting and striving against seemingly insurmountable difficulties that makes life interesting and achievements worthwhile and satisfying, isn't that so? The more we fight for something, the more valuable it becomes. Yet sometimes, and typically rather unwillingly, one has to draw a fine and clear line between success and failure. I was walking that line. It was slowly becoming obvious that, though I was feeling obstinate, I was not on the side of success. Life was moving on while I was keeping myself a prisoner to a moment which had already bloomed and wilted.

Another year went by; she disappeared. In between, I developed some kind of immunity to her disappointing silence. I now viewed the preceding events with an understanding that emerges from failure. In failure, there is understanding, too: perhaps, one truer than a truth which emerges from success. One shouldn't give up in failure, but rather accept the position, at least temporarily. After all, isn't everything in a state of flux and temporality?

Even so, I had not given up hope. I was never the type of person who gave up easily. In most cases, I have wanted to see things to a positive conclusion. But, that out-of-the-blue greeting after a year without seeing her encouraged me to make another go for her.

The next day, I found her at home. As she saw me, she came over and greeted me pleasantly. I heard the little hitch in her breath and the flare in her eyes. But, it was her voice that hit me most. It was the moon's cradled voice that left the oyster bed and had miraculously taken residence in her mouth. I was only able to say hello. And, I suppose, she heard the hesitancy and doubt in my voice. She smiled at me reassuringly. I invited her to accompany me for a short walk since I had some things that I wanted to talk to her about. My whole body responded when she accepted my invitation.

"I have been hoping you would ask me as there are many things for us to talk about. I want to get to know you much better."

I wanted to tell her that day about a love that sweeps everything away in its path with sudden gusts. I wanted to tell her how I felt that day that when she was silent to me and disappeared, that her absence was like a good luck pendent lost.

On a Sunday not long after this, after attending Mass at my local parish, St. Agnes Catholic Church, I was hoping that she might want to spend the rest of the day with me. I was trying to pluck enough courage as we were coming to the point of parting, when she shyly asked a question I so longed to hear.

"Can I come with you, Lucky?"

These words shook me in time and place. How sure I felt it was time to ask her for more: it was time to ask her to be my girl.

"I have been meaning to say this, Lorica..."

I started and stopped, the words crowding into the hollow curve of my heart. And, once again, my mouth would not allow me to free some of these captive words, so long had each waited to be spoken.

She was there, by my side, staring at the ground ahead of us, listening very intently to whatever I was trying to say, maybe knowing the shapes of these words before they could be spoken. I looked at her face; the face I have always tried to cradle in my dreams only to have vanish when I awake.

This was the woman who was walking by my side. This was the woman I knew I was falling in love with.

"The first day I saw you, I was captivated, but that was not the only thing, Lorica. All this time, there was something else that always drew me irresistibly to you Lori...and during the few times we have been together, I have never been surer..."

I paused in order to wait-out how to phrase the next words, to make them sound genuine. My mouth was dry, but my heart prompted.

"It's because I want to keep seeing you, us to be a couple, to be your date..."

As I made those declarations, we stopped walking. In the wires of my mind, the transformers buzzed with the electricity of our love. She was smiling at me with warmth; her undisguised passionate interest encouraged me.

"Lori, I am begging you to give me your time, trust, and someday: your love...I promise my life's worth these."

Feeling like a village idiot, I took a deep breath. Then, I asked her.

"Will you, please?"

It seemed like she had forgotten to breathe, then she said.

"Yes."

And, we became one figure softened and fluid, held in the embrace of our kiss.

RUINS

It took about two months for all the arrangements to come to perfection. It had been two solid hectic weeks for the couple. Now, the wedding was assured of a success. The couple had a little time to rest before the wedding. Joseph went for a little beer to take one drop too many that cheers. It would help him kick-start the celebrations impending tomorrow. It was a moment, a readying of wings about to fly away. He needed some time with his friends, downing some beers and having a last go at the soon-to-be-lost-bachelorhood-times. After all, marriage, like love, is political.

Leona had one thing more to do before making last touches on her hair and makeup. She needed to see her old friend, Shontelle, who had gone through the same experience the previous year. She wanted inside information on what to do and say. She wanted her wedding to be beautiful.

Early in the morning, she finished dressing up and was resting in a deep-brown leather armchair in the sitting room waiting for the car to ferry her to the church where her wedding would be held. Cuddled deeply inside the moment, she took a trip down memory lane.

Following the azimuth back to the beginning, all of these moments she was now enjoying began when she was coming back from her rural home after Easter. At Nyanga's Karingo Bus Stop, the bus stopped to embark and disembark passengers. The old man she was sharing the seat with from Nyamaropa disembarked there. Replacing him, a shy young man boarded there and sat next to her. She later knew him as Joseph, a nice looking young man from Nyatate's Dandadzi Village. During the journey from Nyanga to

Rusape, this young man kept drawn into himself. He was in a world of his own. In a world devoid of any other beings, he blankly stared at the scenery. He seemed half-awake, harrowed by a fate worse than death. He was caught in the eye of his own storm.

Noticing his withdrawn intensity, she caught herself thinking that it might really take the colossal shivering notes of a consort of foghorns to sound the cool depths of this still pond. She watched for a tickle of wind on the water's surface, a reminder, an indication she could use to tell her of the sadness of all that had gone wrong with this man. He didn't show her, by any visible outward signs, that he was aware of her or any other passengers.

The only time he seemed to notice anyone in particular was when he was paying his fare to the conductor. He fished out of his one-man world and darted a glance at Leona. It was a flash, a once-off quick glance. Just as quickly, he withdrew into his cocoon. In Rusape, Leona tried to throw banana peels out through the window and accidentally dropped a peel on his clean black trousers leaving some white spots. At first, he just calmly looked at those spots. But, he was jerked out of his cocoon when Leona started apologizing and trying to scrub those spots off his trousers.

At precisely the same moment, Joseph thought to himself, she is leaning forward, pressing her handkerchief onto my trousers. Is she trying to cleanse me of a lifetime of grief and pain?

The surprising thing to her was that he didn't express anger or anything for that matter, but seemed to be surprised by all the fuss over those little spots and the effusive apologies. It was a whole minute or so before a word managed to slip out of him. He assured her that it was all right. She was listening and she heard it, the soft almost apologetic tinkle. It managed to set down a foundation, solidify the connection, firm up the little commitment now required of her to travel the future which had been waiting its discovery.

This chance had been grasped and, through my courage, she thought, before me opens a road already mine!

Yet, another silence crawled between them. This time, they were now making their way into the gently rolling veldts, home of the sprawling commercial farms which had become so successful there. Those veldts stretched forever until they seemingly touched the zenith of the sky. She counted the trees, the valleys, the bridges as they passed through thousands of them.

This area was different from where they came from. Nyanga, where they came from, was hilly. One couldn't be so sure of what lay ahead of the next hill. It could be a terrifying gorge or another spiky hill. The eye's line of sight was short. The scenery changed abruptly with each new curve making everything to be altogether spectacular. The change, variety, and beauty of the landscape of their home were always surprising. In contrast to the veldts they now drove through, their home country usually settled a quiet awe on all those who drove through. In the flatness of the veldts, one would want to communicate with someone else in order to provide theme and variation to the unbounded and unfettered thoughts stretching outward, inspired by the immense sameness of this place.

However, the environment didn't seem to work its magic on Joseph. He didn't seem to pay attention to it. He was quiet, turned inwardly even, as they moved through the gently lulling veldts of Rusape, where the eyes are bound to look and look and never see the end of things. The mind would be bound to follow the eyes, wondering, stretching, exploring unguarded the zenith of the imagination. One would be left time-traveling, aching inside: unhappy, lonely. Here, sometimes, memories come back, alarmingly.

And, there it was, she saw it: a break in his concentration. He had blinked and moved, as if to loosen his neck. Strangely, she felt the urge to talk to him before he retreated back into his own world. Droplets of words gathered at her lips, hinting to the nature which swirled deeper inside her. Her desire was powerful, a current much stronger than the subtler opening of her mouth, but with no other way to emerge, at least: not yet. She simply knew she had to talk to him.

Belonging to someone is the icon of our human need for connection. It is the expression into which we have galleried all our memories and which has shaped us into individuals. Belonging to someone is the mark that has mapped the man-made marriages of our past, our present lives, and our futures, too. It was this current which stirred inside her and formed droplets of words on her lips. It was this current which bubbled to consciousness just before the words splashed into the world, a world of possibility, much larger than the bus on which they rode.

Here, she told herself, I will offer some few words to this young withdrawn man that due to their utterance could consume old things and shed light on some new things, as well as to wipe away traces of things that should have not been there in the first place.

As she started talking to him, Joseph paid attention to her and responded to her questions with open, sincere, and long answers. At other times, he also introduced some topics for discussion. By the time they arrived at Marondera, they were fairly well-disposed to each other. They had established a rapport.

The hunger of trying to know had been distracting him, though. This was a hunger for the knowledge of an inner threshold. For a brief moment, he had glimpsed at a point at which we dissolve into an insatiable liquid wanting within ourselves. He wasn't yet ready to give words to the threshold. He had only just glimpsed its edge and the abyss just beyond. He had only just grasped that this threshold at which we dissolve is hidden in the hunger to belong.

This hunger to belong is an endless grief. With its load of blistering pins of pain, it propels us through a life. It is a cloying prehensile feeling. He recognized it and was unsure as to how he should proceed. Belonging, he thought in the silent moments between her questions, is a feminine feeling.

The need to belong challenges us to try to know everything about the people we feel attracted to as if we have every right to know other people's troubles, trials and feelings. This feeling, this appetite, ranks out of proportion among the range of human expression. When this hunger has pervaded all ranks and faculties, it makes us to be unashamed of doing things we couldn't have done had we been under normal circumstances. Even our innocence becomes the prey to belongingness' predatory nature.

Would we be ashamed or would we feel noble given the extent to which we pine for or control our hunger for the acquisition of an exquisite belongingness, the kind which we might feel has been eternally denied to us? Would we trade away our innocence for such a moment? Does either innocence or belongingness actually exist as a thing in and of itself? Both are abstractions, after all; probably, they are little more than emanations of the mind. After all, no one can one grasp innocence or belongingness in the palm of the hand and say, "here it is!" Yet, consider the wars fought both within each and every one of us and in the worlds surrounding us over these abstractions. With this meditation, the young man dove more deeply into his reverie.

She didn't give up, though. Instead, she tried to feel, touch, and own her need for belongingness. That was what she hungered for. When the bus arrived at the Forth-Street bus stop in Harare City centre, the place where they were destined to part ways, they exchanged each other's address and contact number. They took these scribbled numbers and letters as a hieroglyphic, a rune, which provided profound notations as to the day's conversations and contemplations. She was very happy that she made good headway against his silent obtuseness and hoped that he would ask her out.

Sure enough, as she hoped, he asked her out. He asked himself out too, giving himself permission to belong to something. He had negotiated that this experience was worth risking a bit of innocence. They dated for about eight months. He hadn't become fully open with her. Yet, Leona wasn't bothered by this. She believed that the true nature of love should remain constant in one person. She became a hostage to this concept of love that, unknown to her, he wasn't even aware of or acknowledging.

Love is always right here before us; we can see it with our own eyes. Our love is visible, because we want to see it. It seems just a finger's length away, so we can't help but to try to reach out for it. Even though it's only a concept, who has ever tired from trying to grasp it? It's a gamble each of us puts so much into, in trying to get a thing. And, this thing, this love, that has always appeared near, a finger's length from us: if we remove the emotional largesse that connects and drives us, then we are instantly smacked with the realization that it actually lives far away from us, a universe away from us.

It was when they had been seeing each other for a year when he started to let her in, like the night's darkness giving way to sun's light. The movement was shaky and deceitful at the start. On one day, there it was: total openness. Yet, the next day, he withdrew. Their relationship progressed with this trend for a while. As time passed, rough edges were smoothed; wounded spots were healed; secrets were exposed. Their relationship deepened.

Were all things out in the open?

There are some things that are too big or too small to be expressed in words. They remain hidden inside us. It is only death that reveals them, returns them to the Endower. There are some hurts too deep for the one who has them to be aware of. They are buried in the deep ocean bottom. Often, they seem non-essential. Yet, years later, they sprout to the fore and infest a pestilence on the tracts upon tracts of achievements and goodness one has toiled painfully to grow.

We know all that we want to know; furthermore, what we all know points to a favorable prospect. After all, we shouldn't worry about things we know nothing of. The inevitable is neither confirmation to the pessimist or affirmation to the optimist. It simply is. Maybe, the argument is a trial in which the case should be dismissed. Perhaps, guilt should be dispatched. Maybe, we are really justifiable in our need to belong, even at the expense of our innocence. Could this be because we have been blinded by the too bright rays of love or because we have been afraid of facing up to our identity? Could love have changed a lot of things? And, were these changes so frightening and daunting that we retreated from the implications love dangled before us? We make a lot of noise in our defense.

"We are human!" We exclaim to anyone who will listen. We excuse our commitment to mediocrity by saying, "they have their failures just like we have ours." Or, we appeal to the great momentum of Fate, a spirit which allows for us to stand by and do nothing in the face of the atrocities of our world. We shake our heads and expound on the horror and follow this sentiment with one which, though designed to unshackle us from responsibility, only damns us further, "We couldn't really have done anything to make that much of a difference."

64

Years later, when the space opens up in our belongingness and when we've already compromised our innocence, we will have to accept the blame. We will have to accept that we hadn't opened our eyes wide enough, that we hadn't cherished our innocence enough. Maybe enough detractors would've helped us to revise our decisions. Maybe the experience of revising a decision might have been an eye-opener to the profound multifaceted complexities of a blindfolded faith, an identity hidden beneath a personality.

This is where Joseph lived, inside an idea he had yet to give birth to, in a personality that was not yet a complete identity. His evolution incomplete, he traded in belongingness, haltingly at first but more confidently as time moved forward. Perhaps, he could have stopped everything, but he didn't. Instead, he moved on and left a lot undone.

Two years down the line, he proposed to her. Burned, scarred, full of fear, Joseph had turned to her, hoping for absolution. For as long as he remembered, she had become the rain, bringing life into his world, cool waters to ease his heart. On her side, Leona only knew she had to marry him, like we all know the inevitability that: once we are born, what's left is to die.

She had come a long way and she was prepared to go so much more further to make their life together a beauty. To both, their life together was an oasis. Calm and settled, each existed inside this bubble, this world of this love. With Leona's answer "yes," they agreed on the day of the wedding. The day had come. Her early morning moment of reverie on that wonderful leather chair was over. It was now time for her to go and have her hair finished.

Later, that morning, she was taken to the church where a lot of people were already, waiting for her and for the wedding. Joseph was there, too, ready to say his vows and to look into her eyes as he made them.

"Looking after each other from today, in joys, in troubles, in riches, in rugs, in health, in illness..."

"Looking after the children in the ways of Christ..."

"To shun away from behaviors that blacken a marriage..."

The "I do," the "I do." In a confident clear voice, she said it unhaltingly, unequivocally. He also said it in a voice that really meant it. At the end of the ceremony, the Priest's words of wisdom lingered.

"Those united together in the name of the Lord should not allow their union be broken by any living person. Now, I pronounce you husband and wife in the name of the Father, the Son and the Holy Spirit..."

With aplomb, everyone in the congregation exclaimed, "Amen!"

"You may kiss the bride."

"Wuhu," "umm," "uuh." In a trance, everything happened to her as if there was a power or some force that was pushing her to say all that she had to say without any qualms or any dissuading thoughts.

"Ululu...uuu...uuuuuuuuu..." The ululation of people and the happiness of the day shimmered out and away from the church in vibrating concentric waves of warmth, sparkling ripples of hope, a chance for human redemption, through all the people were touched by the earnestness of their vows. When it was time, they moved onto the reception which had been planned at their new home in St. Mary's, a suburb of Chitungwiza.

They cut their cake and with laughter, tears, joy, fed each other of their hands.

"Ululu...uuu...uuuuuuuuu..." There were more celebrations, ululations, clanging of spoons on glass. Some people asked them to kiss again, some for this and some for that. The day wore out quickly. In the evening, they were driven to the airport to catch an evening flight to their honeymoon destination in the magnificent island of Mauritius. They were now husband and wife.

A month later after a blissful honeymoon in the island of Mauritius, they returned to their new home. Joseph went back to work at Mercury Real Estate Agency where he had been working as an agent.

Leona was now to Joseph the major streams that gallery our lives, but there were still other minor streams that still connected and built bridges to Joseph's past.

The inside dramas in Joseph's life were now more visceral, porous, and immersive...a field space like the notion of the drift. There was something missed even when they were as closer as any man and woman can ever get.

Sadly, in most cases, Joseph and Leona were just parallel environments, as is so often the case between a man and a woman.

That's how very little we know of the other. In one lifetime, a hundred lives can pass through us. Sometimes, we just watch these lives passing through us, each a tug at a lifeline, a hardening of the heart's landscape. We can see that what we ever loved in another becomes not even a blurred pixel on an old picture of a waning horizon, not even a memory, rather a shadow of a memory that once was.

And, more than the picture, it is the picture which continues to haunt our lives long into the future. Joseph's family life had always been a hell thanks to an alcoholic father. A conflict raged in Joseph between the allegiance a son always feels for his father and the deep anxiety his father's wanton rage had visited upon the life which this man, this twisted man, had given to him. His father could beat a person to death if and when he started in on it. Fortunately, he always stopped short because his mother lashed out at him, all claws and fangs, in defense of their children. Of course, her efforts earned her nothing, but a vicious beating from Joseph's father, her dear husband. And, to her husband, it always seemed a much more welcome substitution. Simply, the family dynamic became toxic, sick anger turned bad and inward. Sometimes, it took her over two months to walk or do anything. One time, he broke her forearm. Another time, she suffered from a minor concussion. Luckily, she was able to get back on her feet again.

When his mother was down, injured from a beating, the family barely survived. Its existence eked by scuttling here and there. Sometimes, they degenerated into a sorry sight, especially the time when it took his mother over two months to recover. They would toil all day long working in other people's fields and ferrying other people's wares in order to raise money for their upkeep and education. If it was not for his mother's intuition, then Joseph and his siblings would never have gone to school.

Knowing that his wife understood the reality of his addiction, Joseph's father always demanded money to buy himself the booze. She started hiding money someplace where no one knew of. No matter how bad she was beaten and no matter the threats issued, she never gave up even a single cent from that source. Her strength was in the commitment that, she would rather drop dead from a beating than to compromise her children's chance of getting a decent education.

Joseph was the oldest of this family of six with three boys and three girls. He remembered Christmas holidays when he spent his time herding other people's cattle. He still remembered the Christmas rains, heavy and stormy, as the rain pelted his back and face. He had weathered the storms toy-toyed and fro-forayed, grouping the strayed cattle, goats and sheep to one place, sometimes clinging to handfuls of the sun's warmth here and there, the wind singing in his knees and his teeth a chatter box keeping a jagged rhythm and dancing a mirthless jig.

What could he really have done on those Christmas holidays? He did not have nice clothes to wear. He didn't have money to buy delicious food like how the other young boys and girls were doing at the shops on Christmas day. After all, he knew the score. He had to help his mother to raise some money to pay for his upcoming secondary school years.

When Joseph finished his secondary school education with excellent grades, he moved to Harare and stayed at the railway platform like so many other homeless young men were doing. It was another hell of a life to survive. Fortunately, he got a job in a week as a garden boy to a white man, Mr. Donilson, in the low-density suburb of Highlands, north Harare. After five months, his boss tried to move to a new residence in Gweru. As Joseph tried to discuss his continuing employment with his current employer, Mr. Donilson learned that Joseph could have qualified for a better job in the first place. It was then that Mr. Donilson helped him get a job at the Mercury Real Estate Agency.

Meanwhile, Joseph's family life didn't change much. In fact, it went from bad to worse. This always saddened Joseph whenever he visited home. Visiting his family always got him. Raw, the experience always peeled and picked at his psyche. His mother had always strived by every possible means to have all her children secure a good future. His father, on the other hand, was getting more and more insufferable. His brothers and sisters had later deserted the family. Their desertions were permanent. During his discussions with Leona, their faces sometimes bubbled up and then disappeared from Joseph's memories. Memories with them became vague, convoluted, obfuscated.

His brother, Tom, moved down-south with his Sesotho girlfriend of South African origin. Matthew, another brother, moved to Plumtree with a married woman from Kalanga. His two sisters had out-of-wedlock children. After finding life too tough for them at their rural home, they moved to the notorious Gonakudzingwa suburb of Nyanga, surviving on commercial prostitution. Joseph knew that, although they could have gotten on well together and supported one another through the challenges of life, they had never really met as a family.

Everything back home came to a head-on sickening horror when he received a phone call four days before Easter. His mother was in critical condition after getting beaten by his father. Subsequently, his father had committed suicide after thinking that he had killed his wife. Joseph went home to witness all of these horrors. His mother was in the hospital. The doctors expressed little hope of her ever coming out of the comma. He buried his father the day before the start of the Easter's holiday.

This whole situation was a pain as sharp as a needle's point. Joseph felt aggravated by his powerlessness to help in his mother's sad demise, her battle against the profound nothingness, the quietness, the deathly silence which was engulfing her. Her memories were now black holes. She didn't respond to anything or anyone. She consumed herself. Her heart was now holding words inside her like an autistic child. When Joseph visited his mother in the hospital, she didn't recognize who he was, but kept starring at him...an empty and blank stare expressing nothing, noticing nothing, feeling nothing. In the face of this horror, Joseph felt himself draining away.

Joseph was in this mood after seeing his mother at Nyanga district hospital until he took the bus to Harare and met Leona, the young lady sitting next to him. That night after getting off the bus and saying goodbye to her, he had looked at her address and numbers for hours hoping for inspiration, for something. And in the quiet hours, he rolled up his sleeve and cast forth, searching around for the keys in the river of his life. It was time to unlock and connect his life to Leona.

Joseph wanted to tell Leona everything about his family tragedy for quite some time. He had even promised himself that he would tell her about it when they returned from visiting his mother. When he returned, though, he couldn't bring himself to say anything, not even a single word about the state of his mother and the state of everything at home. He knew that he couldn't live like this any longer; he had to share the stories with her. He also knew that by speaking out, he would finally let go of those painful memories.

After putting in quite a bit of effort, Joseph managed to open his mouth. He told her of his siblings' desertions, his mother's situation, and that his youngest sister was taken in by their auntie after having been raped by an insane next door neighbor, who was now serving some months in prison. Was there any other way of cracking into halves and splintering into pieces the dense fibers of a life?

Before proposing to Leona, Joseph took her to meet his mother at a rehabilitation centre in Harare. After that meeting, he had asked the question. When he had proposed to her, she accepted his proposal, not even with a slightest hesitation. Rather, she received him with obvious joy. It was love that had concealed its origins and destinations in the many disagreements that they might have had, in layers of distrust and dissatisfactions with one another, in shelves of personal resentments with one another. No, while Joseph and Leona had embarked on a happy marriage, something always lacked. First noticeable in their sexual relationship, this darkness emerged from an even deeper place than that.

They kept their family intact for the first few years and were blessed with two healthy boys. The older one, Timothy, was born in the first year of their marriage. The second one, Timmons, was born two years later in their fifth year together. They were expecting another one. Joseph and Leona hoped that this one would be a girl. At the workplace, Joseph was promoted to head Mercury's Harare Commercial Properties department with a beautiful car and a sumptuous home in the upscale Waterfalls suburb.

Over the years, Joseph had also developed a habit of visiting hideous underworld night-bars, parties, and nightspots. He excused this by saying to himself that there was nothing sinister with what he was doing since he neither got drunk, nor get himself involved in the despicable things savored by the others who enjoyed the nightlife. To him, these adventures were just a welcome refresher to his rather insipid life at home. But are the darker recesses of the human soul's capacity for good or evil ever separable?

Mistrust ends up as an obsession, an insatiable obsession. Was the family he and Leona struggled to build just been an illusion? And, was that the family life an illusory world which was now shattering to ruins leaving them both bare and their lives empty? But, what was it that had exposed that emptiness in the first place? Had it always been there? Was this the belongingness for which they'd compromised their innocence? For Joseph, the answers to these questions couldn't be found in his wonderful home with his wonderful children or between the sheets looking deeply, longingly into the eyes of his wife.

As the need to visit those night-spots developed, the more Joseph's family and work life regressed. It wasn't long before he met someone at those parties. She was the devil incarnate, a soulless, seductive, and irresistible woman. And, like a moth before the light, he fell under that woman's inhuman spell.

As if something had passed between them, they were now two of a kind: uncaring-of-any-humanity, untainted-by-any-religion, and uninhibited-by-any-social convention or tradition-tried-hell. All these civilizing constraints, counteracting values, and institutions rotted away as putrefactions of denunciatory verbiage whenever Joseph grappled with the voluptuously plump, nectar-scented body of Monalisa. A shared emptiness was their fuelling spice. The demon in him moaned in dead emptiness whenever he poured his life into her.

Night after night, Joseph seemed to only get more involved in his pursuit of the she-demon, Monalisa. Frost and fire, their burning sensations were nothing as compared with their lovemaking. Primordial and fierce, it was the burning to ashes of nerves and senses, consciousness and strength. Their lovemaking always left him drained, obsessed. He couldn't get enough. The insatiable demon inside Monalisa was thrusting him deeper and deeper into an emptier, more desolate world.

In her private room in the underbelly of the squalid red-light district, he pawed Monalisa's left breast; he cupped it in his hands and she told him she wanted him to love her right breast in the same way. She told him to suck it in his mouth so as to lick the wild fires of its hardened nipples. He took hold of her right breast as if he was about to swallow it, but stopped to paint it with his breath. His tongue began to make circles around the nipple as he licked her breast slowly and slowly. Like a child about to bite the mother's breast, he raked the nipples softly with his teeth.

Monalisa's world was one of pure sweet delicious pain and pleasure. She told him that she liked what he was doing. She urged him forward. His right hand was still cupping it, caressing it, and sometimes pushing it harder into her chest. When he did that she felt like she was about to crash down and faint with pleasure. She was a raging wildfire, barely able to contain herself. She told him that she wanted his mouth to find her mouth. She slowly directed him downwards. He licked her neck, arms, fingertips, breasts, and nipples again. And again, he moves lower, to the navel, thighs and...his mouth found her crop and got hold of that hotspot of her womanhood. He licked it. It moistened. Her body was now fire itself.

Breaking off, she told him she wanted to love him the way he has loved her. She seized his molar into her hot and dry mouth. She started licking its head and stroking it, casting a spell like the sweet enchantress she was. His senses consumed with pleasure, he couldn't contain himself anymore. He plunged his bristle cawing beak into the slickness of her soft woman. They coupled. With hysterical intensity, they smeared and immersed into a maelstrom of boiling rapids, precipitous currents, and plunges which cared not and were unafraid of any constraints that might reverse it, divert it, or refuse it.

He thrust deeper and deeper into her, pumping harder and harder. She bellowed. She shrieked. She shook like an erupting volcano. She opened deeper, pulling him in, deeper and deeper, wanting more, demanding...wanting and wanting. Wanting more, she slithered...until she couldn't help it any longer, but to cry out.

"Love you! Love you! Love you!"

He battered, cleaved, and drove through with renewed vigor onto the mouth of her womb.

"Now, now, now, Love."

The tight, tight, long slope: He was a barefoot sparrow running across flames, harder and harder, breathlessly...until he lost his footing. He fell, tumbling like raindrops, like the sluggish extrusion of viscous lava, like molten candle wax, spurting-hot raindrops, drop after drop of his manhood rained into her inviting, yet desolate earth. Rhythmic with climactic cyclicity, their unholy love grew, flowered, and was consummated.

He died between Monalisa's silken honeyed thighs paying homage to a renewed, but inverted vow, to a perverted faith and twisted worship. When he was inside her, he felt vaguely aware that it would not be good to reconcile himself to all those tainting antagonisms, values and morals, conceptions and traveled conclusions, of their lovemaking, of their infidelity, of his marriage to Leona. When he was inside her, he touched the primordial depths of the foundation of her animal soul. And, he found that he wanted more.

It started with Joseph coming home in the late hours of night. In the first few days, he managed to fight the urge to spend the whole night with Monalisa. He always lied to Leona that he was spending those nights at work or at social calls with co-workers, but also knew that she knew the real reason. Leona was still afraid of the multiple associations this necessity of change could bring. Confronting the truth can hemorrhage. We mark the scars on our souls as much as on our bodies; give them elaborate histories, as they are the traces of wounds dealt through words, as much the tools of lies and secrets as they are of truth's extraction.

In the seventh year of their marriage, Joseph began missing many days at his workplace. He had been seeing Monalisa for over a year now. He was basically staying with her. He had also sold his car without telling his wife, not even his boss, and barely returned home. When he came home without any money to look after his children, including Cecelia, their third born child, even a few days after payday, Leona went to his workplace in order to be sure of what really was the matter with Joseph. When she arrived at his workplace, she was told that they were also looking for him. Fortunately, one of his colleagues knew where she could find him. That night, she went out to the nightclub her husband was said to frequent. Unfortunately, Joseph had gone on that night to another spot. She didn't give up. She went back the next night.

When she arrived at that nightclub, Joseph was in the process of departing from Copacabana night club amidst an argument with a scantily dressed woman. That didn't come as a surprise to Leona. Joseph was complaining about the waiting game he always suffered at her hands. They were sounding off at each other like dogs, like feral animals tasting each other's limits.

Yet, it troubled Leona that it didn't even register in Joseph's conscience that he was doing that same thing, to her, as he was accusing Monalisa of doing. Leona had a right to go and slap him until he understood how it really hurts to be left alone. But, she fought and stifled the urge. She knew that giving in here and now to the urge would be a spoiler for there were bound to be better ways to deal with such a situation. She stilled her chattering monkey-mind. All that she needed was to be cautious, steadfast, and stay in the moment, to try to not grab too much at one time. Savageness had awakened in her; it would not be silenced with simple rationalisms. A profound crack had split the veneer of her civility. Yet, she knew she was not innocent of her participation in this vortex. After all, she had traded away her innocence for the belongingness of her marriage to Joseph. For that, she would always be culpable.

Leona stayed behind in the shadows of a blue Mazda Etude parked at the entrance to the nightclub. For a while, she followed them at a distance, but just within sight. This woman stayed in the Kopje area. They were making their way to the hideous, cracking staircase of her dilapidated flat. Engrossed in the pursuit of her husband and his lover, Leona, hiding in shadows and behind cars, couldn't even give heed to the fear that she recognized earlier, the moment they had started into this unlighted, dangerous, and notorious Kopje area.

She had to see for herself what her husband was up to. She watched as they opened a small gate and went inside through the ground floor entrance. As she followed them through and got inside the building, she met another whore at the entrance. She asked for the number of the room of such and such person who was wearing this and that kind of clothing with this and that kind of a man. It seemed to please this whore all the more because she readily gave Leona the room number of Monalisa, the third floor on the far west end. Leona thanked her and gave her some 'thank you' money.

On the third floor, she followed the passage to the west. Three doors before the end of that wing, she came to the door marked number thirty; this was the door which she was looking for. She didn't knock; instead, she peeped and listened through the keyhole. There were voices inside which she identified as those of the two. They were no longer angry with one another; rather, their voices had grown intimate. In his voice, Joseph seemed to be in paradise enjoying the promised fruit offered by that cooing bitch.

Leona's world ached and ached as their voices spiraled through the keyhole. Like numbed consciousness, the whispered arguments of little children and their arbitrary voice soundtracks were a mind-burning backdrop to her painful existence.

Prisons have doors and gates. These doors and gates have keys. Each is unlocked by the proper key when the time comes for release. It is our own private cells that do not have keys that allow for us to lock or to unlock according to our own will. Furthermore, it is characteristic that we refuse to bow down to conformity in these cells which we have created to imprison ourselves. Once we forcefully break out of our private cells, we have no wherewithal of returning to the root of what was the right thing for us to be doing. As the proverb goes: broken animals and broken trees are not dangerous.

The black rage that descended and enveloped her was incomparable to anything she had ever felt before. It was as destructive as a raging fire and as inextinguishable as burning oil. And, in this fire, her prison started collapsing. Leona wanted nothing beyond getting hold of that prostitute's neck and squeezing every drip of life from her. She wanted to trample over her dead body until all her anger was sated. She tried, but couldn't hold herself back. Her innocence needed avenging. So, she opened the door which, unfortunately for the couple in the throes of passion, was unlocked.

In the middle of the room, her beast of a husband and his sweating bitch were oblivious of their surroundings. This sacrilegious ceremony of the flesh seemed to have inflated him into some mystical unknown heights, which Leona never thought he could soar into. For a second, she paused, feeling something move inside of her. It was her need to belong convulsing inside of her: whispering crazy things, accusing her, blaming her, even now, for Joseph's actions.

Leona remained rooted at the door as if life at that moment had eased out of her. She was now in a condition in which nothing seemed comparable with her vision of the life that she lived in and believed in. She was no longer aware that she was alive, except for her breath which served as her only physical reminder. How long the moment lasted was beyond measure of a physical clock. She only wanted to see, to peer deeper, to be enveloped by this timeless existence. She felt she was floating with time on a red tide, retreating out of life into a warm dream world where nothing appeared human, painful, or capable of anything that made tears tumble.

But all that she could feel were the hard edges where the cracks of her broken heart zigzagging out from under her left breast into her esophagus and up her throat into her mouth. This cracking went on and on without an end. She smelled the blood coming out of her mouth. She felt it and heard it laboring in her breath. She couldn't scream or weep; her throat only rattled.

Since words can only haunt the space where there has been silence, whatever words she still had inside herself weren't enough to fill this bleeding space and stitch up the wound left from her disintegrated heart, the center of her life.

She snapped awake again; that same deeply savage sense of having been wronged resurfaced again with deathly vengeance. She knew she couldn't call herself away from harming herself with this love that she still had for her husband. She discovered there, in that moment as he thrust his being between this bitch's legs, all that she had given her husband: the comfortable life, three healthy kids, even all of the warm affectionate love despite their poor lovemaking.

Their lovemaking had become the code that shifted and swayed with the mass of the dying minutes of their marriage. It was now a marriage that was in shadows, a marriage cast-about by the magician's wand. All those years of trying and trying to make him happy, all the tears and fears, heartbreaks and aches, pains and hurts they shared. All that had come to nothing.

These thoughts in her mind birthed a struggle, a pain, a dead weight, something distorted and dead like a stillborn. She also discovered she still wanted him; she didn't know why she still wanted him. And, this realization, that she still wanted him, that she wanted to be the sweating slut wrapping him in ecstasy, made her really angry.

Her rage mounted. It had to be expunged against something. She took a meter long metal rod standing by the bedside and started pounding Monalisa's head. When Monalisa let loose a painful and surprised cry, Joseph was taken aback, washed from his beautiful dream. At first, Joseph thought to himself that a man was after him. Joseph disentangled himself from a wreathing-in-pain Monalisa and dashed for the door in order to escape this crazy lunatic. When he got to the door handle, he turned around to see the maniac.

He could almost imagine seeing some tiny sparks of light as he watched the rod descending onto his head. He blinked his eyes to absorb the impact. He could almost feel the strike jarring the very tissues of his brain. He looked at the bed and froze on that spot. It was then that he recognized that it was his wife who was pounding furiously at the almost-dead-with-pain Monalisa.

She was propelled forward in a dazed frenzy, as if her life now entirely depended on pounding this woman who had done her a great wrong. When the other female flat mates came to put Leona asunder, Monalisa was already in the throes of death. They managed to call the ambulance and police in time to rush her to the hospital.

What followed was a sensational six-month trial, which instantly grabbed the media's attention and public limelight.

It seemed people became sympathetic to Leona due to the ill-treatment she had suffered from Joseph. The city clucked about it endlessly. Of course, the outcry was endlessly two-faced. Everyone publicly hated Monalisa for destroying this family, although some couldn't help but privately feel sorry for her, as well. She had almost died that night.

From the beating, Monalisa became mentally disturbed. As a result, she was not much help in the courtroom proceedings. She didn't remember staying at the Kopje lodgings or visiting any nightspots. Monalisa didn't even recognize Joseph. However, when she laid her eyes on Leona, she started crying piercingly and painfully as if she was being beaten again. Suddenly, in the throes of her fit, Monalisa ran out of the courtroom whimpering.

Then, the full blunt of the public's anger focused on Joseph, pinning on him the blame for destroying his family. When Joseph entered the courtroom, he was greeted by boos, whistles, and derogatory quips. He was shunned by his social colleagues and co-workers, as well. He was treated as a pest feeding on the moral fiber of the good of the society, especially by the morally upright citizens. Why had he left a beautiful wife and healthy children? How could others have understood it? How could one have laid his or her finger on something that was as untouchable and private as this, the emptiness Joseph felt in his life? There are some things or happenings that people never really understand.

Maybe, we might really need the profound supernatural mosaic eye to dissect and understand these things. There are certain lines of behaviors everyone is forced to follow. Whoever doesn't follow these rules is a rebel or a moral pest, especially if his or her behavior affects others. This properness emanates from a superficial understanding of our need to belong, one which emanates from our intolerance, and one which has been fostered through time because we haven't been encouraged to look at things with different eyes. Eyes have to be colored in the shade of understanding. Eyes must be designed to look at the reason enough to understand some of these happenings.

Why should we try to understand them? It's certainly easier and clearer not to. Why should we doubt our resolve when we can see clearly, with our very eyes, the very wrongs these individuals have done? It's interesting that we can excuse some weaknesses expressed in some ways so much easier than other weaknesses expressed in other ways.

It was the defense speech that Leona gave in her trial that so touched the hearts of the public. Her speech was repeated in newspapers and people's mouths. The magistrate repeated her speech at his handing down of the sentence, projecting precisely backwards to display as much of her life as was possible.

She talked of her early childhood years in Nyamaropa irrigation area, as well as the killing of her parents by liberation forces during the war. Someone had lied to the liberators that they were conniving and working against the cause. She talked of how her grandmother, old and frail, had taken her in until she died, when Leona was still in her early teens. She talked of her life in Nyakomba, north of Nyamaropa with her uncle, her mother's only brother. She told the court about how, just before she completed her secondary school education, her uncle had perished in the ill-fated Regina Caeli School's bus disaster.

She told them of moving in with her mother's only sister in Mbare Township, in Harare. She told the court of how she had always felt like sad old clothes which are always handed down from one person to another. Her eyes lit up as she talked of meeting Joseph in a bus journey from her rural home, of how their relationship grew, of how she had helped him from that point onwards; giving him a shoulder to cry on, a hand to hold, a heart to confide in.

She told the court of how she always tried to make him happy even during their dating days. How he had always shut her out of his life. She talked of how things started changing during the year of seeing each other when he started opening up. How, later, he had let her in, telling her of his trials and tribulations. She talked about the proposal after many years of solid dating, their honeymoon, its beautiful sugar intensity and satisfaction. The jury saw what it really meant to her.

With grinding teeth, she talked about his dissatisfaction with their sexual relationship. How much she had bled terribly, emotionally in trying to make him happy so that he wouldn't leave their connubial nest. She talked about hours upon hours spent engrossed in trying to understand how and when she had wronged him, the bad things she could have done, the harsh words she had exchanged with him, everything that might have been the cause to this state of affair that was between them.

She shared the intimate desperation she felt as he drifted apart and the endless nights upon nights spent all alone waiting for his return. She talked about the infidelity, the fears, and the tears she had explored, delved into, and counted when the light was on. She talked about the shadows when the light was out. Flitting, smearing, and murmuring in inaudible voices, she had become haunted. She talked of the earliest silent hours of morning when sorrow came to its highest peak, thus causing a sense of dislocation. That, her love for him, became a tight prickly ball whirling deep inside her breast.

She explored with them the feeling of hope sinking low into total misgivings and memory puffing up soft bellows of galling regret. She talked of how she started knitting in order to supplement her diminishing income. She explored how she had given birth to their third child in the streets on her way to the hospital. She explained that she hadn't had the money to pay for the ambulance fees. She admitted to the world that, when he came home with nothing, she had paid for her hospital charges with money made from her knitting. Then, at the pinnacle of the spectacle, she even dissected for everyone present what had made her almost kill Monalisa.

All these things she told the people in the courtroom with a bitterness which everyone excused, but not as an excuse for the deed she had done. That's how it happened and everyone accepted it as the truth.

But, can anyone really be put on trial for infidelity, for failing to love someone as one promised to do...?

There are a lot of other vices that can't put someone under the wrath of the law, for what they have caused: the broken marriages, destitutions, and shattered hopes and faith. Are these small inconsequential inconveniences to be shrugged out of existence as extenuating circumstances in our prodigious march to legitimize our pathological motivations and desires? Does the law recognize these vices and these poisoned moments which can lead to utter destruction of other's hopes and beliefs? If so, then how does the law put right such wrongs?

Leona was given "a year in jail" sentence for aggravated injury to Monalisa. Another year would be set aside, if she was to behave well during her time of incarceration. Did they put her to trial and really compensate for the wrongs she had suffered? Could these wrongs be compensated for by the suspension of some years off the sentence? Suppose they were to suspend a lifetime of years from the sentence, could that have put right the broken marriage, the hurt, the shattered hopes and the resulting destitution of a family?

All right, I am being miserly narrow-minded here. Leona inappropriately took the law into her own hands as if it was right for her to have judged Monalisa by beating her. She was given a punishment for that, but was that all it should have come to? What can make a person stop what he or she has been doing all along? Can one ever stop this never-ending, torment; a degradation that discourages any form of thought, especially constructive critical thinking?

Joseph went down to the darkest and deepest end, thinking that he couldn't pull anything worthwhile or uplift himself out of this degradation. He went from one beer-hole to another. He was sacked at the company. The company took back his house. He was given his dues, which were squandered. In a short while, he didn't even remember having had such money. Left homeless with nowhere to go, the children were adopted by one of his remaining older sisters, a prostitute who was now based in the Kopje area after finding Gonakudzingwa less lucrative.

Later, before the death of this sister, the children, including her own children, moved into the streets. This was a foul tragedy added atop an already despicable situation. Joseph fared little better. He was now the picture of degradation itself: a hardened destitute living from the bins, taking whatever food could be found, and sometimes beating his own children whenever he came across them in the streets. He was nothing, a ghost of his father.

He prowled and prowled the streets and didn't even remember that he once had everything, that he once had a wife, that he once had children, and that he once had a home. Monalisa was insane, just like his mother; both were in an endless battle in a rehabilitation centre with no relatives and no visitors. When Leona comes out of the jail, what might she salvage from this mess? Perhaps, only dusty ruins, shattered and dilapidated fragments, will be the only reality waiting for her.

THUS FAR; NO FURTHER

"**G**ood morning, Sister."

"Good morning, boys..." And, while starting brightly enough on the surface, she frowned darkly before snapping, "...what do you want?"

She was an arrogant and rude person; a streak of cruelty ran through her nature. Sometimes, in most cases in fact, a lot of people wondered why this nun had taken her vows, how she could've been allowed to take her vows, despite her arrogance, rudeness, and a clear violent streak. The parishners even wondered a lot why she was the matron of this godly institution. Why she was, of all the sisters, head of this Mission, Mt. St. Mary's, which was comprised of a primary school, secondary school, hospital and a farm.

"We ehe..e...we have come for eh...e...for..." Edward started, stammered.

"Come off it, boys, you're wasting my time." She reminded us crisply, visibly impatient, with eyes fixed on her watch.

"Uh..."

Before my brother could say anything, she bellowed, "Get the bloody-hell out of here, if you don't want to talk!"

I couldn't stand it any longer. I was up even before she finished her statement. Angrily, I shouted back at her.

"We want our cattle!"

She gasped, gaped, unbelieving at what she was witnessing. No one ever thought it necessary to shout at her. She was surprised why such a young harmless boy like me was taking such a tone with her. In a deadly, icy voice, she sassed.

"Don't you know what to do?"

"But we bailed them only yesterday after..." Edward began again.

"So what?" She broke in, mouth tacked provokingly into her nostrils.

"We can't pay more for them..." I declared thinly.

"Then, what can you do?"

She challenged us, eyebrows raised masterfully to within an unimportant distance from where her hair started on her forehead. Her forehead was now creased into tiny, very tiny innumerable wrinkles.

"Nothing!"

We couldn't help agreeing with her. There was nothing that we could do about it other than paying, of course. It was only a day ago when we paid $5 for each cattle thus amounting to $50 for the 10 beasts we had. It meant we had to fork out another $50 to pay for these cattle in order for them to be released from this locked pen. Maybe we could try to reason with this unreasonable sister. That's what Edward got at this time.

"We are very, very sorry, Sister, but won't you forgive us..., just this once and free our cattle? We promise you..."

"I don't want to hear your promises; rather, you should pay what you owe."

"But Sister, it's God who says..." I tried another tactic, but couldn't finish it as she rowed maddeningly.

"I know what God says. You don't have to lecture me on that because that's exactly what I am doing right now."

She was so angry, so pale, so aroused such that we were so afraid she was going to beat the hell out of us if we kept pestering her. We rushed for the door, stood by the door and waited to hear whether she had miraculously changed her mind.

"Without the money, I don't want to see you here again. Now, get out of my sight, you little rascals!"

We stood our ground a little bit more for we still wanted to reason with her. She rose from her chair and purposely strode toward us. We dashed out and galloped hard for our precious lives as if they now depended entirely on the distance we would put between us. We continued to gallop even as she stood at the door shaking her head vexingly with her hands strangling and estranging her elephantine waist.

"I told you she is..."

"Ok! I know it...you don't have to spell it out for me." Edward laboriously replied. He was breathing gaspingly and heavily, obviously due to the exhaustion from the hard run we had just had. When we were out of the gates, we rested a little, knees bent a little, hands resting on thighs and heads drooping between our knees. We were under the cool sweet shade of a big Acacia tree that overlapped into the road. When we had rested a little bit and our breathing had returned to normalcy, I asked Edward.

"Gosh, so what are we going to do now?"

"I don't know...I really don't know."

"Maybe we have to go home...there is nothing more we can do about it."

"Yeah man, let's beat it off."

"That Sister is a..."

"Please don't say it." Edward said in a quiet and troubled voice.

"Why not!" I thundered.

"Because, eh..." He had stopped mid-sentence. We looked at each other again and then stopped. We realized that we were angry with Sister Clarisse; but rather than focusing on her, we were taking the anger against the other.

For nearly half an hour, we walked home quietly. When we came to the cattle-grid and wire lines that separated the Mission from the Resettlement areas, we saw that the fence had collapsed. The inhabitants of these Resettlement areas had stolen some lines to fence off their gardens. The Mission accused everyone, even us who were tucked far-away in the communal areas of having destroyed this fence. In retaliation, any beast found inside this fallen fence was viewed as trespassing. They would be taken and locked into the Mission kraal as prisoners. They would survive on meagre hay and a little tinned water. Four days inside this cattle kraal turned most into a sorry sight. Only by bailing them out were they to be released. Suddenly, as if struck by a new inspiration, Edward stopped before we crossed that grid. He stared at the grid, and as if by a miraculous turn of events, declared a new plan.

"I am returning back."

I thought to myself that this wasn't really happening, but I could only ask him.

"Where Edward?"

"To the mission."

"Whatever for?"

"Whatever for?" He asked me as if he couldn't believe I could be that stupid to ask such a dumb question.

"Yeah, we have already talked to that damned Sister and I don't see..."

"But, who said I was going to talk to her again?" He retorted.

"I thought e...eh..."

"Then, you thought wrongly."

"Who, then, are you going to talk to Edward?"

"Why, of-course the Priest, Solo!"

"Father Manyawu Edward!" I couldn't help thinking I had heard him wrongly.

"Yeah, why not?"

"Edward, Edward, haa...a...you know you are just wasting your precious time."

"No, I don't know about that."

"Yes, you are."

"No, no, no, I am not wasting my time..." He disagreed heavily. "...in fact he would listen to me since he knows me and likes me so well...he is bound to be lenient."

"Hu-uu."

He couldn't comment on that gesture. Like the Butcher selecting his meat with a fork, I started the probe...the seemingly so innocent yet so painful probe.

"So, you think he would talk to that sister?" I was exuding sarcasm, but he ignored the barb.

"Of course!"

"He would tell Sister Clarisse to release them..., just like that?" I thumbed my forefinger against my thumb finger.

"Just like what!?" He was already steaming with anger. "Does that idea sound so wondrously preposterous to you?"

"Ahh, maybe it doesn't, but nothing of that sort would ever happen."

"You just want to go home." He really meant it, this accusation.

"It's the only thing to do."

"You just can't try anything because it would delay your getting home. Go if you are dying to get home." He threw it and the accusation stunk, but I could only shrug it aside.

"Yes, of course. I am on my way home because I can't be that stupid as to even think such an attempt would be fruitful. Don't you know that he is in it with those sisters? He will tell you that everything is out of his hands, that those sisters have the last word on everything that happens at this Mission, as if he really doesn't count for anything in this world."

"Then, get going if that's what you think, but you will be

surprised to see me coming home with the cattle."

He determinedly retraced his footsteps up the mountain that housed this Mission institution. I crossed the grid on my way home.

When I arrived home, there was no one around. Mother and our three little sisters had all gone to the local shops to buy food items for the coming Christmas day, the following morning. Father, who was home for the holidays from his job in Harare, had also gone to the shops for a beer. I had nothing to do, so I went to the river for a swim and some fun with the other boys who I knew were already there. I also knew I would find my friend, Matthias, at Nyajezi River. They were there, basking in the sun, when I walked up to them. Mathias instantly noticed how dejected I looked.

"Pal, you look so wretched...didn't you find the cattle you were looking for?"

"We found them." I was so downhearted that I barely squeezed the words out.

"So, why this wretched look, King Solo?" He quizzed me so surgically. He had always called me King Solo.

"They have been captured once again."

"What! Not again, no."

He jumped up from his back into a sitting position and stared at me uncomprehending.

Then, he said, "This is pure madness. I can't believe this, by God, no!"

"But, it's the truth."

"Yah...ha...a..." Then, he went into some deadly silence.

I really was lost on what that meant. As if ashamed to have kept me out of his thoughts, he smiled at me, assuring me. He twitched at me wickedly and cringed, visibly angry. Then, he thundered.

"Blood sucking bastards!"

As if he thought I hadn't heard him, this time he hissed rhythmically.

"Bastards! Bastards! Bastards! This has gone too far. We will teach those bastards a lesson."

"What lesson, Matt? We are supposed to pay, Matt."

"Not if we don't want to do that." He declared hotly.

"Then, what can we do about it?"

"Something. There is bound to be something we can do, man."

"Like what?" I prompted him.

"Like eh, uuh...aha." As if he had decided against it, he stopped. Then, abruptly, he said, "Let's go home, King Solo."

I could only follow him. We walked quietly for some time. Before we got home, near our cattle kraals, he motioned me with his hand to stop me from walking past him. He whispered conspiratorially as if his proposal was really that easy.

"We are going to steal them!"

I couldn't just help asking him: "How?"

But, he kept quiet.

"You know it, Matt; they are locked inside the pens. I don't see how we can get the keys from Sister Clarisse."

"There is no need for the keys, war-horse." Instantly, he laughed as if there was nothing, but the fun of the challenge. Then, he started musing out aloud.

"Boy, come to think of it: we could have those keys if we badly want them, even though we won't need them. And, it could be pretty interesting to figure out how we could get them."

"How could we get them, man?"

"We could try Dennis's trick."

"Dennis...Dennis who? And, what trick, Matt?"

"Dennis Mangoro, of course, man! Then, you didn't hear what he did, did you?"

"No, what did he do?"

"Now this is funny..." He started laughing again, a thundering laugh at that.

"What is it?"

Still laughing, he told me what Dennis did during the previous week. When Dennis found his cattle locked inside the pens, he went to see sister Clarisse and demanded that she release them, but was told to pay up first. Then, in sight of all the schoolchildren at this school, the sisters, teachers and the Priest, Dennis peeled off his trousers and underclothes. He told Sister Clarisse that she either had to give him the keys or he was going to rape her in front of everyone else. He made for the sister.

Sister Clarisse tried to bolt away to her place, but Dennis was aware of such a move, so he stalled her and cornered her between the classrooms and the sister's home. Knowing full well that Dennis meant every word he had said, that Dennis was capable of affecting such a deed as he was well-known to be the rowdy type, she threw the keys at him, then bolted for her place.

In sight of everyone, Dennis opened the gates and drove his cattle out and made for home...naked. His trousers were on his shoulders, with the keys of those kraals. I just couldn't help laughing. We laughed all the way to Mathias's family homesteads. Still chuckling, I sobered a bit.

"It wouldn't work with us. She would laugh herself crazy."

"Maybe, maybe not, but that's not important." He shrugged, uncaring of what Sister Clarisse would do if we were to attempt this as well.

"How do you mean..., what can we really do? After all, we are only boys."

"Yeah, but we are wicked boys. Don't forget that, King Solo." Giggling to himself, he changed the subject, "Let's find something to fill up our stomachs."

There was nothing in the kitchen so we went to the granary, filled our pockets with groundnuts and then we crossed over to my family's place. I knew there was some food which I hadn't cared to even look at when I returned back from Mt. St. Mary. After filling up our stomachs with Sadza and vegetables, we then waited for Edward to come back. Just before sunset, our sisters and Edward arrived at just the same time.

"Did you find the cattle?" Anna, the oldest of our little sisters, asked us.

"No, we didn't." Mathias rushed in, but a confused Edward stammered.

"Why, but we...eeh sort of, we...Matt."

"Yes, Eddie, we didn't find them." I declared as I twitched my left eye at him in a conspiratorial gesture.

He saw it, but he still wanted to say something. He looked at me again and met up with my eyes, that same studious determination on my face, raised his eyes to the sky, and then, wretchedly and unsurely, he concurred with me.

"Yea...ah, we didn't find them, Anna."

Anna then reported to us. "Mom said I should give you $50 to pay for them, if they have been caught again."

"Maybe, they were caught again. We didn't look at the Mission." Edward said, instantly pulling himself out of his wretched state.

Mathias quickly added, "I am sure they were locked in the mission kraals. I must have heard Mr. Samaboreke saying that. Anna, please give us the money for we will wake up early tomorrow morning for them after coming late tonight."

"Where are you going tonight?"

"To a marriage celebration in Gwanyan'wanya."

Easily, I supplied this line, our ticket to engage our little plan.

Anna believed us because truly there was Rinos Charera's marriage reception in this village. That's where every youngster was heading that night.

"I hope you don't intend to spend the money."

"Don't mother us!" Mathias warned her.

At the same time, I thundered, "It's none of your business what we do with the money!"

Edward fixed her with one of those dangerous looks of his. She knew if she said another word she would invite a heavy thrashing from Edward. She left without another word or a look at us. We waited as Edward got his fill of the food by getting ready for our evening, especially the necessary night gear which included a wire cutter. When Edward had finished eating, we walked along the way to the marriage celebration, though that's not where we were headed.

As the sun sunk beyond the western Ruchera Mountains we sunk from view, behind Gomorefenzi Mountain (the-fenced-in-mountain.) At around seven, we came to our first resting place just three kilometers from the looming mission. We climbed Gomoremahwe-machena Mountain (a-mountain-of-white-stones). We upped all the way to the pinnacle of this mountain which featured total panoramic views of this Mission. It also had a flat rock covering its top. We rested on this stone, on our backs, gazing into the night sky.

"Old horse, ever heard what Dennis did?" I poked my brother's ribs with my pointed forefinger.

"No...what?" Irritated, but still interested in the story.

I narrated the whole story as if I witnessed it. We all laughed as loud as if we were safely ensconced in our own hut at home, uncaring of what fate might befall us in this dark dangerous wilderness.

"It's a wonderful sky above." Edward said lightly, dreamily.

"Uhu...u...the stars are sparkling so brilliantly in the skies." Mathias agreed.

"Do you see that bright star to the east, there?" I motioned them towards the eastern skies.

"Yes." They chorused.

"Legend says it's a guiding light; maybe, it is guiding us."

"Maybe." Reluctantly, Mathias concurred with me.

"Hu, hu, hu, its trash, trash, trash...useless information." Edward, on a warpath, disagreed.

"But, it's not trash!" Hotly, I disagreed with him, "It's the truth, Edward."

"What truth?" Edward gushed cynically as if he hadn't heard about the legend himself.

"Okay guys, let's rest it a bit!" Mathias brokered a truce in the simmering argument between us. Mathias knew that no solution or compromise would result from such disagreements because no one would be willing to compromise on such arguments.

"What are you doing tomorrow, guys? It's Christmas day tomorrow." Mathias deftly changed the track of our conversation. We warmed to such a topic. After all, it's not every day that a Christmas comes upon us.

"I will be going to the shops...Maria is bound to be there." Edward was first to answer.

"Why do you say bound to, as if you are not so sure?" I asked.

"Why wouldn't I be so sure?" He asked, evasively.

"I don't know..." But, I knew.

I knew all along that Maria and Edward were not an item as Edward would have wanted us to believe. He was crazy about her, but was scared of telling her about his feelings for her.

"She will definitely be there." He declared.

"What would you be doing, King Solo?" Mathias persisted.

"I am yet to decide; perhaps, I would feature at the shops, too."

"Yeah, but let's change the location this time."

"Where else could we go, if not to Nyatate?"

"How about Mawonapadi Shopping Centre this time around, man?"

"But, there won't be a lot of people we know, Matt."

"...and, thus, it makes itself the best of all places to visit this time around, my friend."

"Uhuu...so no one will see us."

We had been going all during the last year to Nyatate to get drunk without anyone noticing us. This time, we had the $50 cow ransom money burning a hole in our pocket.

"So, what do you say, Solo?" He pushed it.

"Ok, we could try it out at Mawonapadi, this year."

"That's great, man!"

"A place for kids one would say, uhuu...u...those who aren't into girls yet...and I would say the greens." Edward contemptuously enthused.

"Hu, hu, hu, buffoon." I was angry.

"But, it's the truth."

"Yeah, whatever...you should know: the world's greatest lover man." As innocently as possible, Mathias concurred sarcastically with Edward. We giggled sniggerly at him and that stopped Edward from throwing in another barb. It was long until our conversations dropped off.

We remained silent, each now engrossed into the daring adventure we were set for that night. Our nerves were starting to get jumpy. At around nine, we started walking toward Mt. St. Mary's mission. By half past ten, we came to the fence that separated the schools and hospital from the farm. We climbed a small knoll of a hill known as Mt. Love because it was a favorite dating place with a lot of young people, especially the children of that mission. There, we waited for the lights to go out from the dormitories. In the meanwhile, we got down to the basics of what we were to do that night.

"You, Edward: you will guard the western side of the kraal so that the cattle won't run through the school." I said.

"Ok." He agreed without a fight as to why he had to guard that part not the other part. "Who will guard the entrance into the hospital grounds?"

"I will." I offered, "So that means you, Mathias, will cut the wires right around the kraal and the gate and drive the cattle out of the kraal."

"It's my pleasure, man, to be thus honored, King Solo." Mathias was truly pleased.

"I think it's okay." I adopted the plan.

"Yeah, but we have to be fast about it." Edward started.

"...and if we are not fast?" I laughed nervously.

"Then, we will be caught." Mathias finished it off.

Suddenly, all the lights went out enveloping the whole place in darkness. We waited for everyone to get to sleep. At around half past eleven, we came down from the hill. We couldn't enter through the main gate because it possibly was guarded. We followed the fence up to its northern gate, past the water-logged Vlei.

We entered through that gate, left it open, and stealthily went to the kraals. I stationed myself at the gates to the hospital. Edward blocked the entrance into the school, and Mathias, as discreetly as was possible went down into the business of the night. Just over a quarter of an hour later, we left the mission looming behind with the cattle and crossed the road into the dense bush to the south.

After having spent over a day as captives and being released to freedom in the middle of the night, these poor creatures were inspired to gallop to the fullest. Rather than slow them, we flew together as birds of the night. We followed the road, deep into the forest such that those who pursued us couldn't see us. Someone must've noticed, though. Two cars, the Farm Manager's yellow Bantam truck, and the Priest's blue Mazda B1800 truck, went back and forth with nothing to show for their effort. When they had gone back for sure, we re-crossed the road and entered into irretrievable territory. Thus, into safety, we focused the beasts on the path home.

We couldn't help looking back. The whole place was now alighted. We supposed the mission boys and girls were trying to mend the kraal and restock it with those other cattle we had released together with ours. We knew that never again would our cattle be captured again.

With no danger coming from behind and no hurry for that matter, we walked our cattle, being led home by the recent risen moon, ocherous as a ripened gourd. At the second hour of morning, we arrived home and locked the cattle into their kraal. Like the heroes that we were, we went to the marriage party. Not only to celebrate the marriage, we surely also had our own celebrations to make. We were excited for the coming sun.

It was already Christmas day.

MANGOYI – THE CAT

A week before I finally proposed to Mangoyi, my best friend, Bothie, came to me and asked about my intentions on Mangoyi.

"I love this girl and I would like to propose to her if you are not interested, Charlie?" he said.

I answered him sternly, "No Bothie, no; Mangoyi is mine, boy."

I replied to Bothwell with so much anger and jealousy, that I had never felt for a girl.

Fuck doubt and all purveyors of doubt.

Mangoyi had become a commodity, a possibility requiring contracts and transactions among the boys. I told my friend that I planned to tell her about my feelings that coming weekend when we would be spending the whole weekend together at our Youth congress in Seke rural area.

But my friend didn't take 'no' for an answer and went behind my back and proposed to her before I got my chance.

It was even more difficult for me to be compassionate with Mangoyi when, during the following week, she told me that he had already proposed to her, too.

Should I have told her, "Please, don't love him?"

Should I have kept silent?

Mangoyi had those stunning big white eyes and they burned into the spirit inside me whenever she looked at me. Or, perhaps it was her eyelashes which were dark and heavy which lulled me into a trance. Most likely, her magic was in the fragmented light, the yellows, greens, and browns which her irises reflected into anyone brave enough to look into her eyes. My friends used to call her

"Mangoyi, the Cat," simply because her eyes resembled those of the cat.

It was her friend, Shingirai, though, who made it all the more complex between us, Mangoyi and me. This Shingirai, this Mupotanzou tree, was surrounding me, ruining my chance to graze peacefully in Mongoyi's presence. This Shingirai had cast her eyes on me, a year before we met and tried to become a perimeter fencing Mangoyi from me. Since she had something to enclose within her bending, supple stem and branches, she had made every effort she could to discount me to my Mangoyi. She openly told me on more than one occasion that which I just didn't want to hear.

"Mangoyi would never ever date you, Charlie."

"Why not?"

"Because it's me whom you first loved and you shouldn't have loved my friend as well."

Shingirai knew that all she and I had together was sex, one sweaty night, and that we were never a couple and would never become one.

It was her, Shingirai, who was the one who had come over to my place with lust in her heart and had insisted on spending the whole night with me. Our entanglement was her design. I let her stay out of loneliness and need. But, I recognized that it had been a mistake, somehow wrong. The next morning, I knew it would never be repeated.

Never.

Loving Mangoyi had my total attention. And, in this attention was a discipline. To show my discipline to my sweet, I was required that I feel as if I were wearing my internal organs outside in the open. It was at Rockwood spiritual centre, in Hatfield Harare that I first felt inside out.

It was prayer day, a couple of years after I had met Mangoyi. By that time, we were getting along fine. She had called me several times asking me to come over to Rockwood for this prayer day. She had even come to our house to encourage me to come over to Rockwood since I was and always have been reluctant to travel outside my parish area for church related activities. I am not much of a traveler, really.

Mangoyi had smiled sweetly as she said, "I have a gift for you. Charlie and I want to give it to you at Rockwood,"

Seeing my confused look, Mangoyi repeated, "Come over to Rockwood, be with me throughout the day and you will find out what it is, Charlie."

I came to Rockwood to be with her that day, and not for the prayers. If all I wanted to do was pray, then I could have done that at home. It felt really good that Mangoyi had asked me to come out and spend that day with her.

From that day onwards, I believed in her. I believed that she loved me, not that other Harare guy about whom I had heard gossip. When I arrived at Rockwood, I was so happy to see her waiting for me at the gates and so happy when she took me to meet her Auntie. I was glad when Mangoyi asked me to stick by her all day long.

When she eventually brought out the present for me in front of her Auntie and told me that I was the best friend she liked so much, I wanted to believe that Mangoyi had said the best friend she had ever loved, for that was what was in her eyes. I nearly died with love for my beautiful Mangoyi that day, for making me feel warm like the sun kissing my back. I wanted to touch her that day, to hold her in my arms and make love to her.

Her Auntie saw that: she demanded to chaperon us throughout that day. She sat between us and fragmented the magic bonds that were pulling us together.

By the end of the prayer day, I looked into her eyes. I saw my own distorted reflection in her eyes. I saw my own brokenness in her eyes. Even though she was so beautiful, I also found out that she was less than perfect, and that I was far more tragic than I had ever imagined.

By the end of that prayer day, I couldn't help gazing deeply into the eyes of the child that Jesus was holding in his arms in the picture she gave me as a present. I was so scarred upon recognizing that child as a reflection of me, of how I felt for her, of my trust in her, my vulnerability.

It must have been all of that or none of that, or even more...

Was it because of the other gift she gave me, a keychain made of braided black leather with a silver ring at one end and a weighted Celtic knot, also in silver at the other end? Mangoyi never told me it was a love knot...

Did I want her to hold me in her arms, into her being, into her heart like the way Jesus was holding that child in the picture? "Let the children come to me", Jesus was saying in the picture. Was she also asking for the children to come to her? And, was I the child here?

I became very afraid!

At the bus stop at Caledon shopping centre, I didn't seek cover from the rain when the sky opened. I just stood besides Seke road and let the rain drench me and let the spirits in the rain wash away those thousands of feelings that I had stretched over me. The frustrated thoughts and feelings washed down by slathers of rain into the ground. When the rains had passed, I felt a little bit cleansed and started trying to flag down a bus or taxi to take me home. You see, I was empty. Loving Mangoyi had sucked every prayer out of my heart.

I later heard from Shingirai that Mangoyi was still dating that Harare guy and later-on that she had started dating a local guy. That friend of hers even told me that all that she ever wanted was for us to be best friends. I started to believe Shingirai, even though I knew there were layers to the things I had seen in Mangoyi's eyes that day at Rockwood.

When I confronted Mangoyi, on another fateful day, about this local guy she was said to be dating, she told me that guy was just a friend. I believed her even though I knew she was just lying. I knew that Mangoyi was no longer crazy for my company anymore.

This guy used to come around every Sunday to pick Mangoyi up at the church, bringing her presents and food. Later, he started coming to the church and I had to watch my Mangoyi spending every moment with him. She told one of our mutual friends that it was this guy that she had feelings for, not for me. So, I started by hating this guy and then ended up hating Mangoyi too.

Later-on, I reconciled with my friend, Bothwell, whom I had fought with over the right to date Mangoyi. The two of us collectively hated her and this guy as the guy took her for a ride. The guy was such a player; yet, we still hated Mangoyi and laughed at her when the guy dumped her for another girl at the church and added insult upon injury with the things he said about her. Even though I knew she was hurting badly, I still hated her and didn't have any comforting words for her.

People are animals. The only thing that guy wanted was to have sex and piss me off in the process. When he accomplished that, he dumped Mangoyi.

A couple of months later, when I visited my mother, she showed me the picture Mangoyi had given me and which I had left there on accident. I told her to keep it. My mother asked me why the word, 'Mangoyi' was written on the back. I told her that I had deleted her actual name and put this name instead, that I wanted to forget the name of the girl who had given me the picture. My mother understood.

I gave the keychain to one of the girls I dated a couple of years later as a gift, but didn't tell her that it was a love chain from another girl. Some years later, when I returned home again and saw that picture, it wasn't painful to look at anymore.

I burned holes in my memory where my precious Mangoyi had been, where my love for her had been, where she had once lived. Every night, I swept up all those memories like leaves and burned them. In the morning, I scattered the ashes into the wind. Little by little, the map of my moments with Mangoyi no longer equated with the map in my heart. Little by little, I began to desire this distance growing between us, Mangoyi and me. As wounded as I was when she left me and too much in love, I hoped that one day she would come back and we would be together.

But, I know that this is not to be.

A SILLY STORY, HEY!

"What would you say about this, and what am I going to do about it?" I was saying this to Aggie.

"How could I reply to something I don't know anything about? What is it that you are asking of me, Cass?" Surely lost on this conversation Aggie is, the start of which. She is a very close friend of mine. We have been through a lot together.

"Oh yeah! I understand what I have been doing." I concurred with her. I have started badly- the conversation.

"Do you?" She asks me, unsure, whether it isn't intentional on my part. She always accuses me of being all over the landscape in my stories and evasive, especially on some things very personal.

"Yes, asking you questions that you don't even have an inkling of whatever they are asking for. Ha-ha! I am being stupid, unintelligible, ain't I? I should have told you the whole story and ask you questions later. "

"Yes, that's what you should have done first, Cass." She sighs, heavily.

But, is it a story as such? I can't ask her that question. I don't want to be accused of being evasive again.

"You know those late autumn days, Aggie?" I start again, tying in another narrative thread.

"Autumn days have always been good by me, so what's up with those autumn days, Cass?" It's good that she is still smiling: beautiful teeth grabbing whatever light they could out of the restaurant's light.

"It was end of April; one of those horrible, waning or are they as frightening as such, I mean autumn days, Aggie?"

"You should know better than to ask me. I think I only want to hear of whatever happened to you, Cass."

"They should be, Aggie ..., what, with the fiery cold winter just knocking around the horizons. You feel like you can do yourself a whole-lot of good by wrapping yourself in some cotton and put yourself in a nice warm place..., maybe in a warm fantastic dream to be unwrapped by the dawn of the coming spring."

Aggie is shaking her head, already exasperated with me; with these throw-ins in my story; 'the philosophical take', she calls them. But, she can't say that aloud now. She knows this would throw me on another philosophical flow and it would be difficult to stop me once I start on another one.

"What of this day?" She asks in a striated voice. It might be the cold; the July colds that are making her feel so rattled. She continues, and there is now an emotion I don't really place in her voice. She is always protesting against the colds, all throughout the winters. But, the funny thing is we are in the restaurant, drinking tea, yet it seems the hot tea isn't sipping away this sense of being perpetually cold in her. Outside the restaurant I knew people were moving in waves, even in these colds of July, they formed a total movement, a wave complete into itself.

"You know, Cass, I really do hate the cold, you know that, getting so miserable, being cold all over my body especially my toes." She folds down under the table as she touches her toes, as if they were really that cold, and needed massaging to warm them up. Then, she continues when I ignore this toes, hiding-behind-the-finger; take of hers.

"You said end of April, you could be wrong, Cass. After all, which end of April are you talking of? Nevertheless, all this isn't important, Cass; rather I simply want to hear whatever happened to you, please, please..."

Now, that's irritating I am thinking; to be told that you don't know what you are talking of, as if she was there when everything happened. Yes, she was there, I know that. But, I also know the day I am talking of, or else she might as well go to hell. What if she doesn't want to go to hell? I can't ask her that, though. She prompts me more, in unbelief.

"What if you are, indeed, confused, Cass?"

"All right, Aggie, I think I am boring you flat-out by harping-on, what do you call them?" I ask her, raising my left eye, inquiring.

"Silly nothings!" She is flat, unencumbered by my displeasure, in her replies.

"Silly nothings, hey!"

"Yes!" She is forcefully there in her 'yes'. She really means it.

But, is to love someone as silly as those silly nothings? Don't you think that I have every right to talk about them since it is very silly of me to have loved? Granted that I am silly to have loved but do I deserve it? I have to ask her this question, I am thinking to myself. It deserves an answer from her.

"Do I deserve it, Aggie, do I really deserve it?"

"What is this, 'do I deserve it', Cass? You should simply stop being this irritatingly evasive and tell me clearly what you want to talk to me about."

"Maybe I do deserve it, Aggie; I really thought that I deserved it." Should I simply accept everything thrown at me by life?

"Buzz, buzz...," Aggie is blowing her nose, but I can hear she is disagreeing with me. Aggie always blows her nose whenever she doesn't agree with me. I can't ask her,

"Are you refusing to swallow your tea, Aggie?" I can't even say, "Lucky you, you still have the liberty to choose." So, I start afresh, telling it from that autumn day.

"That autumn day, Aggie, I didn't want to wake up, in fact, why in heaven's name should I wake up every new day?"

"Why, yet another big nettlesome day to see through, hey!" She tries to lighten things with this statement, and take a good gulp of her tea, play around with some tea in her mouth, feeling it, tasting it, and warming her mouth, enjoying herself...

And, I am thinking about this day that; why didn't I keep asleep until my back was sore and aches terribly? There are a lot of whys in this life, I answer myself. I continue, not rattled by Aggie's attempt to light up things.

"We don't seem to find answers to all of these whys, but rather, we follow the dictates of good reasoning." I know to Aggie, I seem to be replying the question she didn't even ask

"What's this, I don't seem to be following you?" I want to tell her that it is obvious, that she is not following me, but I can't because it's a rehearsed line. I don't want to use it.

"I am saying we have to wake up and perhaps some of the reasons might crop up later-on whilst we are awake."

"Like which ones?" She takes me on this time.

"Like Rudo?"

"Rudo, Rudo Nyawera, you mean Rudo Nyawera, do you?"

"Of course, like Rudo, love; it summarises everything, Aggie."

"Love...ho?"

For me, it isn't for the word love, but what Rudo the person has come to mean to me. Say you did spent the better part of last night thinking of her; thinking that you have finally found the love of your life. What might you call her, and why am I asking you this question? Silly me ho-o! Say you have been thinking of all the things that you want to do with her, with a real girl, with your lives together; I mean..., forever?

"Now, we are talking about Rudo, Cass?" Aggie asks, sarcasm squatting thickly in her question.

"You want to ask me that, too, even something so clear, Aggie?"

"Yes, Cass." She is smiling in a funny, sort of sideways smiling-insouciance's smile.

"All right I'll answer you. I am talking about love for keepsake, marriage material. I am talking about when I had finally found the mother of my kids. Yes, I am talking of Rudo Nyawera, Aggie."

"Oh! Wedding bells..." She asks.

"Yes, I hear your sarcasm friend, and from that marriage, Aggie, I wanted a trailer-load of kids, as many as was possible. I wanted so many so that I could pin them by my knees and spank them in numbers, rather than just one at a time. How many kids do you want to have, Aggie?"

"We were not talking of the number of kids we want to have, friend? What does that stuff about kids have to do with this story?"

"Well, well, well, I have started on it again!"

"Yes, you have."

"Ok, ok, ok, you have me there, maybe I am silly, yes, that I am. Yet, I like to be silly given that thinking about kids is as silly as falling in love. All right I will stop this thing about kids. But, in that night in question, I believe that at some point during that night I must have stopped thinking about the kids and doze-off, Aggie. But no, I am not going to doze in the middle of this sentence and story, neither are you."

Actually, she is not dozing, but is distracted with something else in her tea. She is staring into her cup of tea as if the story is lost inside the cup. She doesn't even respond to this but stays focused in trying to unearth the story from the tea cup. After a while, I am drifting of, in my mind with the story into one of those philosophical journeys of mine. I am talking to myself this time so I just plough through without being disturbed.

Tell me; you Aggie, who still want to insist that I am awake how I could see myself, remember I am in bed, chasing a whirlwind and surely it is a whirlwind. Could this have happened when one is awake?

Ok, you are saying that I must be dozing off, that I am already dreaming. No, not that, for I am hearing what you are saying, so I can't be dozing. And, to make sure that I have said this to myself, I shout it all the more.

"I am not dozing off, Aggie!" It invokes a reply this time.

"I didn't say you were dozing, did I?" It's like she is waking up from something, else, from some dream.

"Funny, the whirlwind had a head like a person's head, Aggie. At close quarters it appeared like that of Lucifer we have seen in our children's books. As I ran faster and when I thought with a little bit more effort I could reach it, it appeared a lot farther away. Far away, it appeared like Rudo's head and face..."

"The Rudo that you loved, the girl that you wanted to marry, Rudo Nyawera, do you mean, Cass?"

"Just think of that, friend. The girl I wanted to marry. Am I frightening you or do I have your attention now?" She is quiet to herself, and I want to think that she is now following this story. Should I be hopeful?

"Ok. Ok, ok, I stop this needling!"

"What did I say?" She protests.

"It's obvious you are disappointed with me?" She just shrugs her shoulders, in a Gallic shrug.

I don't know how I am feeling like in this dream. I have never known. Do you know how you felt like when you were dreaming? What am I dreaming of? A whirlwind, Lucifer, Rudo, and a lot of kids; the kids that are crying a very hurtful sound- there are not the kids that I want for myself. These kids could take a lifetime to raise them into grown-up men and women. Are kids really horrible when they are crying? But, I continue.

"Later on, was I still dreaming, I don't know- maybe, but someone laughed!"

But she ignores this, and I repeat it.

"Yes, someone laughed, Aggie."

"But who could have laughed?" She can't even hide the irritation in her voice, but I ignore it.

"Yes, someone was laughing, Chengetai, my older sister." She always has a good laugh and I really do like it when she laughs. It's like you get this feeling that the world is worth laughing at, that it really is a funny world. Aggie is laughing; a half laugh, a defeated laugh, and I ask her.

"Don't you think so too, funny like jokes and don't you want to laugh too?"

"Laugh, at what, Cass?"

"But, this dream wasn't funny to me, Aggie. How could it have been funny?"

When I am thinking I have finally found the love of my life, dreaming of a trailer load of kids, but that is not as silly as such. In the dream, there is a reddish glow to the western sky, like a smouldering fire that only needs one breath or gust of wind to make it burst into flames. And, the eastern sky is crammed with stars twirling dangerous onto me like a bullet in the dark night. I suddenly wake up, with a start, in the middle of the night because I have also heard someone laughing. The owls outside are working up a bumpy rhythm as they sit star-wise in their tree of science. I don't find that laughter funny. Instead it is eerie and harrowing.

"What was that dream about, anyway?" It seems she hasn't followed me, that she hasn't realised that I have moved into the reality of the day I wake up to this dream. After all reality, mind and thinking are just words.

...Sister Chenge is sweeping the floors and, my younger sister, Sharon; she is a whole lot cuter and mischievous, is making another go at the old man. She always has a lot of mischief up her sleeves and father gets the full-blunt of her mischief most of the times. Momma isn't around nor Stephen, my older brother.

"Where on God's earth have they gone to and who could I confide in? Why is it like a doomed-in-hell day and where is Rudo?" I am asking myself, loudly.

"We are back at Rudo Nyawera, at her place..." Aggie answers me.

"Of-course, she was at her place, you are correct there, Aggie. But then, what was that dream about, and what was really wrong. Something must have happened."

"Really!!"

That day; the morning was confidently settled in the sky, the sun, a constant rope to bind the worlds of night and day, in this morning sky, was an expansion of dream, and the focusing of work. I take our cattle up to the fields. I am in a little rugged lane up to these fields, the lane is like a line, and the middle of the line resting on a forked prop of hazel grass, still greenish. It is the time of the year when there are no crops in the fields; the land is brownish red as if it's slowly burning underground, a blank. I can't really focus. The grass is already browning and some trees are bare of leaves. The leaves in the tall trees are just going dry and beginning to turn red and deep gold. In times like these, this harsh turn of the year, one can't help start musing about how times and things change in this winter's death, so quickly in such surprising ways, why. Only a few months ago, it was spring, with a lot of greens springing up everywhere. I am not only thinking of this spring but, of Rudo, the coming into my then lonely life of her.

It is in October when she accepts my invitation for a date as the earth's slow tilt had returned us to the sun. Since then I have been a slave to love. Since then, I have felt what love could be. Since then, I have always looked forward to tomorrow knowing that it would always bring Rudo to me as lovely as the day before. I sometimes couldn't believe that we had been seeing each other for a couple of months and that I have already started thinking of her as my wife and looking very much forward to marrying her the coming summer.

Here I am, talking of that old, old story and institution and if people love each other don't they marry? I love her. I really did love her. If I am not sure of this then I am not sure whether I am still breathing or not. And, I am thinking.

"Please don't keep staring at me as if you don't believe me. If you want to doubt me please doubt me on anything else but please don't doubt me on this one. If you doubt me on this one, then you must really be silly. I guess you don't want to be branded that?"

But, it seems Aggie, with her you-never-know-look still thinks we were not in love, and what can I say to this? She is still staring at me with unbelief in her eyes.

Maybe that she might really be that silly, but what would you say, Aggie; to the fact that I thought that they were the only things to live for, always loving and living for Rudo.

What would you say, Aggie, to the fact that Rudo accepted me not because I had so much to offer her, but because she felt that I truly loved her and that she felt the same too. What would you say, Aggie, to the fact that the previous afternoon she had accepted my marriage proposal without any compunction. What would our

Aggie say if I tell her that all the people that I confided in expressed their satisfaction with my choice? At least, would she believe me now?

"I had a date with Rudo at our usual secluded spot, close to our homes and fields where disturbances were bound to be minimal. I wanted her to myself and I also wanted to tell her of the previous night's dream, Aggie."

"What is this dream, dream thing, Cass?" I can even hear her whines, not aloud though, in her replies. I also want to tell Aggie how I really felt about Rudo, but, I try to sympathise with her.

"Am I tiring you with my tirade about love?"

"Yes, you are, friend."

"I am so very sorry, but won't you ask me what happened?"

"Happened!"

"Yes, what happened?"

"But, I know everything." She doesn't really say it verbally, but her raised eyebrows say it. I ignore her. After all, how am I going to tell you; you who are not stupid and silly, especially you? How am I going to tell you that the moment that I rest my eyes on hers that I see that something has changed overnight between us? That I am already living in the dream again? My vision sort of blurs, I can't seem to discern whom I am talking to. How am I going to tell you that instead of being greeted by a warm embrace, a sweet torrent of little kisses, that I get a cold and foreboding smile?

"You should have asked Rudo what had happened to her." Aggie says to the silence between us.

"Yes, I asked her that question, but I also asked myself what had happened to me too. Don't you know about the previous night's dream, Aggie?"

"Dream, dream, dream, are you crazy? Is there an end to this dream, dream thing of yours, Cass? Rudo neither knew what

115

happened to her nor to you! Is that what you are trying to say, Aggie?" She raises her hands, defeated, placating me.

"Am I trying to be dramatic, am I?"

"I never said that."

"You imply that by your gestures?" She shrugs her shoulders, again in a Gallic shrug. She seems to have mastered the Gallic shrug for this specific purpose.

But, in this day, when Rudo is laughing, I tell Aggie, it is kind of phoney; it is not the kind of laughter that I have come to associate with her. She is hurting inside or maybe it is both of us hurting in the insides? When I try to talk to her of what I think is of interest to both of us. I am talking to someone else who is not even there. She is thinking of something else or maybe someone else?

"You are being so very unrealistic!" Aggie protests heavily this time.

"Ho-o, ho! That's all that you can say to all that I have been trying to tell you, 'Unrealistic!'"

"Yes, unrealistic, Cass."

"But, who could have been realistic in love? Not me, not even you, then who, Aggie?"

"You yourself, Cass, you were but not even you, no?" She attacks me, offering back the doctor his medicine. So, I try to earn a bit of her sympathy this time.

"I am so very sorry that I have burdened you with my so unrealistic notions. All these words and time, all these thoughts and feelings have all just been a waste. I can understand that I haven't moved you." I didn't want her to fake sympathy on me, though, because I don't deserve it and also I am bloody unrealistic and boring, am I not?

"Yes, you haven't impressed me with your story, friend. I am sorry, as well. I don't think it was with all this gibberish that you have been throwing at me. I know you were hurt but it's been time now, friend. You should let it go, friend, somehow you have to." Maybe she is correct, time has to move on. Time moved on.

Time moves on like a tide swiftly to some new destination. Life after a sad affair, or death, maybe! Some people are afraid of talking of death but I am not, not even by half as I fear that other destiny. Which one would you fear yourself? Maybe death since death is not as stupid, silly and as unrealistic as me.

"It's been five years since."

"Since what?" Chimes our Aggie as if she doesn't know what I am talking. She can ill-afford to ask me this question because she's been a trusted support all these years. Some of you still have questions. Ok, fire them!

"Did you cry?" Another asks,

"Did you try to talk to her?" Another ploughs in, a bit blindly,

"Did you try to engage others to talk sense to her?" A chic says,

"Were you hurt?" The blunt one blunts in,

"Are you still...?" All these questions and, how am I supposed to answer all of them! What would you ask, you; you who have been quiet all along, you who have maintained this terrible silence and composure as if you feel sympathetic to me, do you, do you really?

Sympathy hey! I have lots and lots of it and they all feel sympathetic to me; Father, Mom, Stephen, and the ever laughing sister Chenge who has meanwhile taken to brooding. No, I am not lying, and even the mischievous Sharon isn't anymore mischievous, especially to my face. But, would their sympathy help?

Here I am, jilted by someone I have come to look forward to as the truest love of my life, and one offers sympathy? That's not what I wanted. I wished for more. I wished for the truth. What truth?

That really this isn't happening to me. Yet, it was! Yes. I am unrealistic. I tried being real, behave sensibly by all outward counts. I also tried everything reasonable to make her understand, and when I fail to change her mind I accept it as over. Isn't this being very realistic?

But, I can't help crying in my heart. This is very realistic too, isn't it? Sometimes we do cry, even tears of blood. Sometimes, it hurts, pains, as if we are going to be a wreck forever. It gets very confusing when you try to stitch together a few patterns to make it understandable, and you don't find the answers. Yourself. *Myself, but.* Yes!

Here and there, I start seeing some changes. When I can spend days without thinking of her, and when, after two years, I can think of her as someone else's wife without hurting. Yes, and that's what she's been for the past few years, not that she still is. With that, I need reassurance. And, I have it from Aggie. Oh, come off it! Rub off that knowing smile from your face because what you are thinking of is not the truth. Besides, Aggie is happily married to someone she loves, aha-a. It seems she could love, just like I loved.

Silly hey! And, some more questions…

"Did you forget her?" And an older friend asks,

"Did you forgive her?" And is this different from,

"Are you still feeling hurt?" We are still there with,

"Do you still feel the pain?"

"Are you still in…?" Oh! Aha—a! You ask a lot of questions but there is only one question that you are afraid of asking me. Like I said, it's been five years.

It has also been five bad years for her too. Being married in the first year, having a kid in the next, the third year the man she's married to turns out to be drunk, and a womaniser. What do you do when you discover that you have married for the wrong reasons? When you got married you found them interesting and a little bit different to Cass, I mean Casterns, of this world but not now? You also discover that they loved your money instead?

Some day, five years later, it is a warm fine spring day. I am walking my two dogs, a shepherd and a terrier, one of my favourite passions over the years. Broken hearts; don't they find some substitutes to distract them? Dogs!! I can see that you are surprised, aha, and confused, but dogs are a lot more faithful, aren't they? Here I am talking about ideas on how to fall out of love with an adored one. Maybe you could have carried on as if nothing happened to you, and you could have talked of her as just that someone who waltzed through your life; leaving no hurt, no disillusion, nothing! You are the realistic sort!

You, who have been silent all along; maybe you could have taken a marriage counsellor's career, aha-a! You have all the necessary trappings and trimmings since you also were once jilted. People would listen to your advice, really! Songs of experience are a wise thing to listen to. You could specialise in affairs gone sour, but what advice would you have given? Perhaps, that people should avoid falling in love since it can be mighty-painful when things fall apart. That might be jolly good advice, silly, no, yes, wouldn't that be?

That one, those other ones too, they look the types, talkative! They could have gone all over the world crying to as many a shoulder as is possible about how this other girl maltreated them. Only that they might end up falling in love again, and the prospect of falling out of love being an unexciting one, ha! Yes, it is. Suppose whilst you are with another woman, Francesca, and think you have finally cried Rudo out of your system long enough to forget about her. You are in a jovial mood and, then at the entrance to the restaurant, there you spot Rudo. There, she is coming into the same restaurant you are in. You were telling your Francesca about Rudo, and she was telling you that you have to let Rudo go. But now, Rudo is there at the entrance to the restaurant. It seems she has refused to go and you can't chase her away from the place. You can't even run away, yourself. But, this is not what disturbs you. You are surprised; not by seeing her after all these years, but by the insanity of feelings you still have for her.

Remember, I am not really at the restaurant, no, but I am just walking my two dogs. A Sheppard and a terrier....

Ha!

A silly story, hey!

THE BLACK GOAT

We couldn't have faced this woman, not if we wished to live to see old age. Nobody ever dared faced this woman and lived another year. She was a witch. Not the kind you would hear about or maybe conjure in your visions because you think you have just seen someone that looks like a witch. Everyone knew it

This was not the only thing that everyone knew about. Everyone also knew that this witch, fearfully known as Mbuya Kamuture, could turn herself into a goat when she went out for her night's call. No one cursed this goat, talked to it, talked about it disrespectfully, or beat it. A lot of people did one or another of those things and woke up complaining of an unknown ailment. It could only abate after they had offered their contrition and apologies to this goat.

No one ever volunteered to stand up and do something about this goat. On my own, I wouldn't have tried it, or even thought about it, not even dreamed about it. With my cousin Rutendo's instigations and dares, though, nothing was sacred. With him, there were only a few things in which I remained uninvolved.

"You know, Tino, the two of us are capable of anything, you know that?"

I didn't answer him. It was just a statement. It could have meant anything, nothing or everything at that.

"Are we not?" He quarried.

When Rutendo started like that it always meant he was trying to fast-talk us into a very dangerously zany and nasty adventure. I raised my eyes inquiring about what it was, but couldn't read anything in his eyes other than glimpsing a hot shaft of determination. I reluctantly gave in.

"Yes, we are Rute."

"Yes we are; we can do it; we really can, you know?" As if he wanted me to say yes again, but to what? Then, he asked me, "Are you afraid of anything?"

"No!" I replied to him emphatically. It was a question that dared me to say or give-in to the notion that I was a weakling as compared to him. This had always been our world of contention. Neither of us wanted to accept that he might be inferior to the other. I would've really rather have bowed down to a day-old tot than to Rutendo, not that privately I considered myself an equal match. I am not really mad enough to dare to compare myself with him.

If the truth be told, I was afraid of him. He seemed to border on a kind of insanity. Not only for that, but he also seemed to know that I was scared of him. So this became an attractive avenue for him to channel his taunts and challenge me with these strange endeavors. It seemed to give him a lot of pleasure to include me in his tantalizing insanities. Unfortunately for me, I couldn't have pre-empted myself out of these endeavors. If I had even tried, then he would have had a field day with me. He had been silent for some time as if he was afraid of saying what he meant to say. So, silly me, blind of the hook that would take me out of my world of safety, I asked him.

"What's the matter, Old Mate? Is something bugging you?"

"You know nothing does that to me, in fact, ehe..."

"So, why this sullen silence, Old Boy?" I gorged him, enjoying my short-lived superiority.

"Nothing...uhu...u...lets beat the bloody-hell out of Mbuya Kamuture, you know, sort of, you know?"

"Oh no, no, are you crazy?" I gasped fearfully.

"Yes we can, you know, sort of, you see." Shrugging his shoulders uncaring of the mysterious worlds Mbuya Kamutures could affect against us.

"No! No! No!" I shrieked repeatedly.

"Yes we can, we can, we can..." Stomping his feet hard on the ground maybe in order to make me believe in this insanity.

"But why?" I still wanted a reason.

"We can." As if he hadn't heard a word of what I had been saying.

"But why, Rute? You know she is sacred."

"No it isn't, it's just garbage and old wife's talk. You know that. It's nothing but goat head soup to us, Tino."

"But, we will die."

Even saying those words had taken such a lot out of me because of the ultimate finality of the prospect. Chilling words, chilling prospects, but...

"Woo...ho...o...I can read fear?"

"Please, Rutendo, stop this madness!"

"Yeah, I am madder than everyone else in this entire universe. I am also the bravest person you can ever come to meet, you see." Poking my chest with his forefinger he added, "...come to think of it, my little chicken...for the record: you will never ever measure up to me, chicky-chicken."

He said that proudly, beating his chest, posturing all the more about his greatness as if he was really that great. I had seen enough of this kind of posturing from him in the past. I could have walked away and left him to his own madness. But, to compound matters for the worse, he started imitating the clucking and squawking sounds of a chicken as it fled from capture.

He was so near. I felt like slamming my fist onto his large, happy face. But, I couldn't follow through. The last time I did that, I had entertained one hell of a walloping. There was only one thing I could do. I just had to humiliate him. I had to bundle him with his goddamn high-horse attitude. I had had enough of that.

"Yes, let's do it boy." I took up the challenge, dispassionately.

He started jumping around and about, one leg stomping the hard earth, ululating, raising his fist into air, clapping his hands, sometimes imitating a cock readying itself for a fight..., and whistling other times, enjoying himself to such a stand-still.

I could only do likewise, but I didn't know why we were celebrating rather than dropping dead because of the infamy we had incurred in sentencing this Black Goat to a beating.

"Yes! Yes! Yah! I knew you could be counted on." He gushed happily and beat me rather hard on the chest. I could only chuckle...rather frightfully.

After another round of riotous celebrations, and this time no longer subdued on my part, it seemed like I was now infectious to the mood, he stopped rather instantly, rather quietly, as if he feared being overheard by the Black Goat; he said.

"Let's go to the gardens."

"How do you know she is coming?" I whispered.

"It's just a goat, Tino. Please stop calling it a 'She' as if it has turned into some human form."

"No, Rute, you know that this is not a goat."

"Come on, Tino! It is..."

"How do you know she would be coming to the gardens?"

"I just know."

"Answer me, please. How do you know, Rute?"

"I called that bloody-thing a witch this morning when I saw it at the fields..."

"What happened?" I enquired gloomily

"Nothing."

"Nothing! How do you mean nothing?"

"Ok, ok, ok, it just stared at me rather stupidly with those funny eyes."

We remained silent, looking at each other fearfully as if we had heard some movement, an unwanted eavesdropper hiding in the tree's shadows and listening to our conversation.

"It will come." Rutendo authoritatively declared.

That decided it. We found a strong rope made of fiber and, after rummaging around, another smaller rope of the same making, a piece of clothing, and a box of matchsticks. Rutendo also took his barbed-wire sjambok. I took mine made of chain. We made our way to the gardens on the banks of Mwenje River to the north of our homesteads. Rutendo was joyously whistling to a song I hadn't heard of before.

I knew what it really meant. It meant we were going to have a riotous afternoon. That didn't seem to inspire me somehow. I was still sullen. It wasn't difficult for Momma to figure it out as we met her coming from the river where she had gone to water the garden and fetch some water.

"Good afternoon, Mother."

"Afternoon, Mwanangu Rutendo; afternoon, Tino."

Before we could sidestep past her, she inquired.

"Where are the two of you headed towards?"

"To the river." Rutendo smoothly supplied the answer in a way thus allaying any questions or reservations Momma could have had. All the same, his slick answer didn't seem to stop Momma from cautioning us.

"Don't get into trouble, okay boys?"

"No, we won't." Rutendo lied, and then addressing me he said. "We won't, right Tino?"

"No, we won't."

I faked his commitment and enthusiasm. Momma kept staring at me and I knew she didn't believe a single word she heard. I started rounding a small stone under my feet to distract myself from wilting under my mother's unbelieving stare. At last, she said.

"Ok."

She left us there and proceeded with her journey home. Likewise, we proceeded with ours. Rutendo whistled another maddening tune while I dragged my feet with a sullen expression stubbornly supplanted on my face. Something indescribably funny was happening to my stomach. I shouted at Rutendo to stop the singing because somehow whatever he was doing was getting at me. Silently and finally, we reached the gardens.

We removed the thorny branches covering the outer layer of the gate, left some thorn-less branches still intact, but covering the gate. We opened a gap wide enough for us to crawl through and entered, leaving the gap for our quick escape. We inspected the wall of branches, twigs, leaves and poles walling the perimeter of the entire garden. We found it was still secure. Then, we looked at the beds of vegetables, onions, carrots, tomatoes. We found that nothing had been touched.

Instantly, we glanced at each other because we had heard the unmistakable bleating of goats on their way to the river. We smiled at each other conspiratorially. I was happy that an opportunity had presented itself for me to prove that I was braver than Rutendo. He could beat me when we fought; and secondly, he was a year older than me, though we were in the same class. It was in only these differences that I was prepared to accept his superiority. I really had to have something to beat him at.

We took cover behind the shrubs that were a few paces from the west of this gate and lay on our stomachs, ears intently listening for the coming of our guest. Five minutes got by, then ten, twenty, half an hour, then nearly an hour. We couldn't take anymore of this waiting so we agreed to rise up at the same moment. Without looking around, we galloped for the gate.

We wanted to look outside the garden to see what had become of the goats we had heard an hour before. We came to the gate, peeped through the branches. Only, those other goats that had grazed with the Black Goat, had decided, in the meanwhile, to bask on the sands by the river's banks. The black goat's absence was conspicuous enough. Where could it be? Where else? Where, where, where, other than being there by the sands or in here, inside the garden? We came to that same conclusion without even talking or looking at one another. Instantly, at the same time, we turned around. There, standing in the middle of the vegetable beds, standing irreverently, amusedly at where we were hiding, we confronted our nemesis.

We stood there gaping, eyes trying to reach out and have a closer look, maybe in order to assure ourselves that what we were seeing was just an illusion, not the truth. Time stretched on unimpeded, flying on the wings of a darkling wind. We seemed gripped in the forelocks of this sinister wind which enveloped and

enmeshed us into its darkness and brood. I started fighting it...,
struggling, pushing and shoving. With an audible sigh, the moment
gave way. I looked at Rutendo and I saw him fighting that fear too.
I also looked at the Black Goat and now it was staring at us. A
bottomless, bleak and wane stare...the goat's eyes stared through us,
unblinking and glassy.

I looked into its eyes again and saw that they were the lightest
blue, almost ashy-blue grey, which contrasted strangely with the
goat's charcoal black colouring. I knew why people were so afraid
of its eyes...It was their blank soulless stare.

"What's the matter with you, Buster? Are you chickening out?"

I didn't know who I was addressing, but my two companions
instantly responded. The black goat seemed to see us as if for the
first time. It rattled insidiously low and started moving towards us.

Rutendo gurgled, "ohoo...no, no, no."

Frozen there, Rute stood transfixed, greedily gulping air, and let
out the oddest sound. He belched. At first, I wanted to flee as fast
as my two little legs would carry me, then I realized that I didn't
have to do that. I stopped and looked at the goat again. Then, a
thought appeared inside of me. I knew then that Rutendo was
going to run even if I don't, and that would have meant I would
have accomplished nothing. That his superiority would be once
more evidenced. But, this would not be the story on this day.

Rutendo had dashed swiftly to safety at the far end of that
garden and waited to see what would become of me. The black
goat kept coming determinedly; it stood in front of me, and stared.
I stared right back at it. I stood were I was, blocking it from
escaping past me through the opening. We stood for some time
staring at each other, like two enemies sizing each other's strengths.
Then, as if it had decided that I wasn't worth enough a match, it
gave a sigh which was in no way any kind of relief. Rather, it
sounded as if it was sorry. Side-stepping past me, it tried to bolt
away for the opening, but I wasn't having any of that. I dived for its
hind leg, got it, and dragged it inside.

127

For the first time in my life, I heard it bleat more like a goat. This weakness seemed to propel Rutendo into some action. In a frenzy of some sort, he flew to where we were, gave it one hell of a wallop with his bare hand. It yelped a little and that drew a chuckle of mirth and amusement from Rutendo. He very much wanted to do it again, and had raised his hand high when I bellowed, "Get me the ropes!"

In the middle of the arc, before he slapped it again, he stopped, razed me angrily with brown glowering eyes, thought about it and vexingly gave in. He went without a word to take the ropes, which we had left behind the shrubs where we had been hidden earlier. I knew Rutendo would now respect me. Standing my ground and catching this monster made Rutendo start looking at me differently, even with a little flicker of fear. It is one thing to decide on an incredible thing like that and another to do it, especially when everyone else is fleeing. It makes a young boy look invincible and unafraid, even a little sacred and insane. I knew from then on that I was the unchallenged leader of our team. I knew that Rutendo would listen and carry forward whatever shots I call. It felt so beautiful.

He brought the ropes and we gagged the goat with that piece of cloth we brought along. We forced it into its mouth and pushed it to the far end of its mouth. Then, we took a small rope, drew it inside its mouth to the far end of its jaws thus dividing the upper jaw and tongue from the lower jaw. We squeezed the rope tighter and tighter until it seemed like it was halving the head into two portions, then tied the rope behind its horns securely. We reversed the loops into its mouth, crossed them, then up, covering the lower and upper jaws together and tied those loops securely together. We took the longer rope, tied the goat by its neck and dragged it to the strongest tree near the right corner of our garden where no one could see us. We tied the ends of the rope to the tree securely so that the ropes wouldn't give in. Then, we started beating the Black Goat using branches from the Peaches Tree at the middle of the garden. And, so, the fun started.

We wanted to see who would break as many sticks as was possible. One could only count coup when he had expended the stick to the point that it would no longer be possible to hold it. We climbed up the tree, broke our branch, climbed down, sometimes jumping, then start beating the Black Goat as it circled the tree trying to avoid the beating. When we finished with the stick, we threw it on our heap without stopping to count the coup. Over and over, we dashed for the tree, at first with hilarity, and then the moment took another twist. We were now men on a mission. We had to destroy this witch.

"Let's use thorny branches." Rutendo suggested

"No, no, no, it's not good enough for Mbuya Kamuture; rather, let's use our sjambok."

"Yes."

Rutendo dashed for them. We started on another circular dance again, and another one, and then another. Right around the tree, this time, when the goat circled and brought itself to a stand-still position, we didn't release it; rather, we checked how securely it was tied to this tree. We lit the matchstick, dried wood and dried grass and made a fire under it. As it was roasted alive, we started beating it, fuelling the fire with more wood; then, we beat it some more; we, again, fuelled the fire, beat the goat over and over...until the sun set. We simply had to kill it. This time, we took very large poles and pounced on it. It still refused to die. The night got darker and darker. The Black Goat's back, its legs, head and stomach contents were now a slowly oozing mess, but it still did not die. We gave up.

Fuming with unrequited anger, Rutendo went near it and looked into its eyes. Then, abruptly, he started laughing, howling laughter, and spontaneous. I joined in. We didn't know why we were laughing. We just didn't know.

Without even closing the gate, we left everything as it was and started on our way home, laughing whenever we looked into each other's eyes. They just looked funny, colored now to a lightest blue shade like those of the Black Goat. When we got home, we didn't say much to our parents, but rather laughed and laughed, stopped, talked gibberish a little, then laughed and laughed.

That night, we entered into a journey. The following day we were still on that journey and by night's fall we came to our destination. After a week, we returned home. We returned home to confront the news that there was a termite's mound where the Black Goat had received its punishment.

We also heard that Mbuya Chikayi died after groaning and whining with pain for several days. That did not surprise us. We did not laugh. We were not afraid anymore for we had been healed of the laughter. Our eyes didn't look anymore fun, no.

We knew we had killed the Black Goat and suddenly it felt all right again.

LET HER GO

"You will never really be happy if you can't let someone take care of you and to learn to love them in return, Conrad."

The pain in her words made me cringe. Even now, those words still tug parts of my waking consciousness every now and then, especially when I think of what might have been between the two of us had we been a bit more mature about things. But, I have always been foolish, and letting go was all that I was good at doing when I met Candice. It had been a long journey coming to that point in my life and there were a lot of moments, now memories, which I had to let go.

The first day I saw her, I was going to church early in the morning. In a hurry, I wanted to get to the church in time for the start of the Mass. The parish priest always started the Mass at exactly 8 sharp. It was the first time I remember her, although she later said she had known me for years.

So, the two of us had to snatch some bits of conversations as we were rushing to get to the church in time. I really liked her straight away, but wondered if she could already be spoken for. She told me her name, Candice, and that she was staying in Guyo Street, a couple of streets from where I live. She later told me she knew where I lived for she was with the other youths of the parish when they came over to pray for me when I was ill a couple of years ago.

The first day I met Candice, I really felt attracted to her, but I had been attracted to other girls before and all that had come to nothing. I was also involved with another girl at the church, though it wasn't going well. I also knew that: when I fall in love, I end up getting hurt badly. So, I am wary of this happening again. By the time we reached the church, I wanted to date her, but was afraid. So, after church, I didn't look for her. In fact, I avoided her altogether.

I saw her later, a number of times afterwards, at this church and in my local area, but I only said hello and exchanged some pleasantries. There was no doubt from these chance encounters that she really liked me, that she was still very much looking forward to more from this connection. She told me later that we were too long in coming together, that she had pined for me like nobody's business all that time.

Three months later, during April, Candice came to have her hair done by my next door neighbor. When I saw her, I joined her at the neighbor's house, and we talked while waiting for the next door neighbor to finish another customer's hair. When I asked her for a date, she told me straight away that she would like that a lot, but also that she was seeing someone else. She says her relationship with that someone was sour, but that she still needed some time to sort it out. I didn't want to wait. So, I told her that she could sort her issues with the other guy, but in the meanwhile we could get things going between us. We agreed that she would take three months to get disentangled.

I asked her who the other guy was. She told me the guy stays in Cranborne, in Harare. Over the next three months, we were seeing each other; I discovered that she wasn't entirely truthful with me. Every time she would come over to my place and I would accompany her home, she behaved weirdly when we were passing through the next street. Deep down, I sensed that there was something wrong, but she said there was nothing the matter. In those first three months, she also made a lot of excuses as to why she couldn't see me at times, or why I couldn't come over to her place at other times.

Although my family knew that this girl is a player, since they had seen her a lot of times with different guys, they didn't say anything. They wanted me to figure that out on my own. What they didn't know was that I had some clues as to what was really happening. What Candice did was to figure out my schedule quite well so that she could dally with other guys during my working hours and after eight o'clock in the evening when she knew there was no possibility of me coming across her. But, one evening, after eight o'clock, I decided to buy some things at the local general store, Mai Getty Truckshop, at Zengeza 2 shopping centre. When I got to the store, I saw Candice standing by the far counter with this other guy who lives in the next street, and whom I had suspected all along. Candice ignored me so I went to the far counter where Candice was and I stood next to her as I asked the shop assistant for the couple of things I came to buy. Candice still continued to studiously ignore me and left with that guy. I followed them a couple of moments later. They went to the guy's place.

The next day, she phoned me and didn't even try to explain anything about the previous night. She behaved normal as if there was really nothing the matter. I couldn't take this deceit so I exploded and told her to go to hell. She tried to lie that the guy was the one whom she was with before we started dating. I told her that I knew who this guy was, that he lived in the next street. She lied that the guy was her sister's boyfriend and she was singing like a canary on steroids trying to convince me that there was nothing really between her and that guy. Even though I knew she was lying about all that, I accepted her explanations because I was not yet ready to let her go.

Over the months, we were seeing each other; I had grown to like her a lot. The truth was she was fun to be with, but I also knew that deep in my heart that I was just hoping for things to work, even though I knew it would not last.

The next months were molten times. We exploded with feelings for each other. We made love every moment we could find. The sun shined on us. The moon smiled at us. She overwhelmed me with love, attention, and interest. Somehow, she took hold of all my fears and doubting grandmothers. She magically relocated all these doubting grandmothers to the back of my mind. I began to believe that I was the only one she loved. I was hooked into her, addicted to her in every sense of the word. I also believe that the other guy was just a ruse. I was so much in love that I had stopped entertaining any other doubts.

In October of the same year, she asked me what I had in mind for her that coming year-end. I asked her how she felt about me and she told me that she was prepared to go to the grave with me. If she was wearing a mask over her face when she said this, then this was by far the most impressive artwork that I have ever had the opportunity to see.

I asked her about the previous relationships and whether she had cut the other guys. She told me she hadn't spoken to any of them for months; yet, the insecurity washed over me again. Candice promised me that there was nothing between her and these guys. Again, those grandmother doubts of mine sprouted back to the fore of my mind.

Over the years, I have discovered that I could love with all that was in me, but also that I could easily turn my back on any relationship that makes me feel insecure and inadequate. This is who I am; so, I asked her to first cut it out with the other guys before I could start talking of settling down. She argued that she had cut it out with the other guys that she hadn't seen them for over six months. That wasn't good enough for me.

Any other guy would have taken her at face-value and married her straight away. I have always been stupid and insecure when it comes to love, that I have to feel secure before I can commit myself to a girl. But, since the opportunity to meet a girl like Candice doesn't come so often in a lifetime, I wanted to hold onto her. She seemed to accept my explanation, but somehow something had changed between us. It was like the spark and eagerness had dried out of the relationship.

I agreed totally with her statements when she said that I was insecure and afraid of committing, and that I can only be happy when I let someone love me without having to make a commitment. But, it's one thing to realize that and another to change my entire life's disposition on these matters. It is also one thing to know that I am losing someone who has become the centre of my life, and another to figure out how to hold onto them and keep them from drifting away.

By the end of the year, she had drifted badly. She got back with those two other guys and probably many others. Most of the time, she confided in me about these other relationships. At first, I believed she just wanted to get back at me and make me jealous. Angry, I asked her why she was doing that, behaving in this manner. She told me that she doesn't believe in being faithful to one guy in a relationship anymore.

For some time after that, I talked about ending this nothingness between us, but I couldn't bring myself to do that. I may have been locked into my fears, but I understood what was ravaging her heart. She was more similar to me than she could've ever imagined. The secret of her behavior, like so many of the behaviors which define our lives, was locked in a story. In a quiet moment between us, she let it slip. Before she met me, she had dated another guy who was such a player. One day, she visited that guy without telling him that she was coming. When she got to his place, she found him making love to another girl. Witnessing this betrayal affected her over the years. Since, she admits: it has been difficult for her to be faithful in a relationship.

Understanding this ate whatever feelings that I still held in my heart for her. It troubled me for some time that I had some kind of a defective gene or a heart scar that drove me to empty myself on heartless girls like her. Like the Kenny Chesney song, "Baby, you saved me," I knew that no matter where my reckless soul would take me; I was going to be fine. So, I focused back on the things that kept me balanced and stopped focusing on what made her throw me off.

Later on, I started dating another girl from the local area. As it happens, one day, Candice saw me hanging out with her. Candice refused to see me again after that. I'm sure that this was proof of some kind of self-fulfilling prophecy for her. The situation was proof that she was right in arming herself in unfaithfulness as a method of keeping safe from hurt. It didn't really bother me, though, because I was on the roll again.

In life, there are times when we roll and other times when the teeth of our gears get stuck and stop. When we are rolling, mistakes and cares get obliterated. The clock ticks inside itself, being what it is, and it's as if there is nothing to worry about. These are great moments while they last, but they never last forever. When the wheels stop, we start to rethink things, sometimes in a maudlin sort of way. There are times when we regret things; situations that we feel offered us more if, somehow, we could have done things differently. These not-so-good memories, with their haunting alternate endings, rub. The friction lasts longer the more you think about them.

Sometimes, the feeling haunts us so badly that we want to go back to correct whatever we did wrongly. But, we also know that going back is no longer an option. What has been done has been done. All that we can do is to just try by all means to keep going hoping that someday everything will be fine again, that the gears will mesh once again into a delightful synchronicity.

There are some loves we really want to work out well, but not all relationships can work out the way we want them to. The tough task is to let them go when we have to, if we can't make them work well. We know that our lives are defined by the series of choices that we make. When we are growing up, especially in our teen years, we often try to hold onto relationships and bleed them until they become unattractive in order just to stay together. It's because our feelings are so powerful at that age. As we mature, more we come to know that beauty is in enjoying relationships while the feelings of love and unity are strong.

I have also come to realize that these memories light up the dull moments of our future lives. These moments allow for a worthwhile reflection for us to look at who we are, why we are the way we are, and how we might find a way to continuously develop. When we think of our loves and how much they had come to mean to us, we learn something of our own maturity.

Light on, Candace, I wish you well...

IN FATHER GANYIWA'S HELL

It was Christmas Eve. People had poured in their thousands, from all over the suburbs of North High Fields; in fact they would count to over five thousand, to this Christmas Eve Mass, at St. Agatha Catholic Church. It was just off Willowvale road in Throgg Morton Avenue. The Mass would start at 8 at night, and would drag up to 11, and then people would spent the rest of the night and morning singing and giving praise, celebrating the birth of the Savior. It was the norm, so people had come in their thousands. A lot of them were young people. It was like a night out for the young of this church.

There was always a lot of talking. The parish priest they had was fairly new and young, around 34 years. So, he seemed to want to talk all things in only one Mass. He would repeat and repeat things, and it would bore like dust mites. Father Ganyiwa, Fidelio Ganyiwa was the parish priest of St. Agatha, and he was driving himself apoplectic, talking, in his homily.

"Beware of the devil. He is waiting, stalking you. He is in your heart, do you hear him, do you feel him, drumming in your chest..." His assistant priest, the old ailing, Father Carry, was off this night, recuperating from heart bypass operation. So, father Ganyiwa had full control of the Mass. In his mind control was intelligence.

Saverio touches his chest. He feels the beating of his heart. He asks himself, "is my heart the devil". The father had just said the devil was in his heart. He didn't know what to think now. Saverio is sited besides his girlfriend, for a year now. It is dark on the fringes where they are sited this night. Saverio and his girl, Tsitsi, like many other young naughty people of this church, liked those darkened fringe places, in this church's yard where the mass is being held. The Mass is being held outside because the church building wouldn't have accommodated the five thousand plus parishioners of this church.

There were young people around him talking, not even listening to father Ganyiwa's sermon. They could just talk anyway, whether the priest starts on his long unwinding homilies or not. It was just a convention, coming to these Masses. Saverio was sometimes touching Tsitsi, groping her a bit, for nobody bothered that side. It was like in the movies, at Rainbow Cinema Theatre, in central Harare.

"Young man, sited over there..." The priest points towards Saverio.

Saverio feels like the priest had pointed at him, so he is touched by guilty. He removes his hands from Tsitsi's small back, and groans in frustration. "You are making noise there. It's the devil in you who is making you do that. You are flirting and touching each other there, it is the devil in you that is doing that. God is going to judge you. He will cut that talking mouth, those groping hands, and those evil and coveting eyes. He will burn all these in hell..."

Saverio tries to listen to father Ganyiwa, but all he could feel is the heat-soaked late evening summer's air, in his nose, in his breathing. It is a very hot humid night. The air is too heavy for 8 at night. Breathing is difficult, sweat trickling slowly from his armpits as if it is broad daylight. He tries to follow the homily, to ignore the heat, to ignore his want to touch the small back of Tsitsi's. He feels defeated. He is cursed. He feels he is surely going to hell. He wants to touch her, he is fantasizing of cuddling her...and he is in the church. This shocks him. He is the devil. The priest's words, jagged little points, pieces through his mind, cutting him into guilty potions,

"You will all perish. You will all be going to hell. God is going to punish you. In a very huge fire, you will burn for all eternities..." Saverio imagines such a fire.

Would it be hotter than the night is? If it is going to be hotter than this night, then it sure is going to be unbelievably painful, he muses. But the priest said everyone was going to hell. This is the hell of father Ganyiwa, everyone? Even the power mongering Parish Chairman, sited in the good seats on the front, even the well known Songs Conductor, Mai Chitembo, whom the people have been gossiping was having an affair with father Ganyiwa, himself. Even the thieving Church Treasurer, a young man, unmarried, who was always failing to account and manage the church's funds; all these were going to hell. The funny thing was the priest would say that, in his homilies that everyone was going to hell, but when he finishes his sermon, he would associate with these people; eat at their places, and play snooker with the young treasurer, go to the night bars with the parish chairman, associating with these people who were surely going to hell. Saverio knew there will be thousands in father Ganyiwa's hell.

The fire should be easy to deal with!

Father Ganyiwa's hell bound person, in his head, possesses a feature Father Ganyiwa doesn't like. When this person performs, or tries to live his life, he produces a performance Father Ganyiwa is not happy with. But rather than focusing on addressing the features that is affecting this person's performance, his solution is to damn this person into hell. The features and performances would remain unchanged in this hell. Hell, what the fuck, Saverio shrugs, uncaring of this hell. He starts groping his girl. Tsitsi looks at him with cow's eyes, and smiles at him, encouraging him. They were surely going to

140

hell, so why wait, why bother? Our life is a play of good or bad, returning at last into a void, so why make an effort? Saverio muses.

All these bodies, in their thousands, lighting a fire was always the favorite sermon of father Ganyiwa. Every Sunday he would find a way to make it part of his teachings. In all his homilies, he was always saying everyone was going to hell, with the exception of himself! Father Ganyiwa stands like a moral rock!

Later, Saverio had been dozing as the priest droned, drooling on and on, about hell. It was time to give his followers the last prayer and blessings, after they had received communion, but instead, he had started talking on about hell, again. He was rumbling on, as the heavens cracked open into half. It was a huge, heart rendering explosion…and it rumbled for a minute, stopping father Ganyiwa in his rumble. He jumps from his chair and makes for the underside of the Alter table. For a minute, he stays under the table, hiding away from his monster hell.

At first Saverio almost thought it had really happened, Heaven and Hell had arrived. Father Ganyiwa's hell had visited them, all too sooner, but he realized it was thunder. The sky and the air had changed, as jagged lines of lighting exploded and cut the sky, a giant noisy breathing, in flashes of pink. The rain ploughed down, without much warning. Father Ganyiwa realized what was happening, so he got out from under the table, and continued with his hell sermon, protected from the rain and thunderstorms by the tents and veranda of the church, so were all the important people, as a huge torrent was hitting harder, swamping the people. People near the church building made for the church, in order to avoid being blanketed in this opening ocean of thunderstorms, but the priest bellowed, in a huge voice,

"No! Nobody must leave their places for the church, or even for home. The Liturgy committee, please make sure you have closed all the church's doors and the gate. Everyone should sit or stand in the rain, and embrace God's blessings. Rain is God's blessing. He has forgiven you all, for your sins. Embrace God's grace. You should be strong. God is great...."

Father Ganyiwa continued sprouting venom in his talk, as thousands of his followers tries as best as they could to deal with the painful pointed drops of thunderstorms and rain. Those who had umbrellas tried to open them, but there were beaten down and broken by the thunderstorm. There were just a few trees people could seek shelter from, after the same priest had directed for all the other trees to be cut, a couple of months before. The rain beat the people down. People tried to take as much as they could, but it started with those playful youngsters, shouting bad things to the priest, telling everyone that the priest was a fake, immoral, and a bustard. It developed straight off into a drone of an angry tornado. All the other people started scolding, shouting and threatening to beat up the priest.

It reminded Saverio of the Sundays they would use the church for the 9 o'clock mass. At St. Agatha, every Sunday they would have three Masses. The early morning Mass, at 7, was for the sections of this parish. The 9 o'clock Mass was for the youths, like himself. The 11 o'clock Mass was for everyone else, especially older people. It was the 9 o'clock Mass that was a problem, especially if father Ganyiwa does the 7 o'clock Mass, which he will always finish late. He would always finish it way after 9, thus when the young people entered the church for their Mass, they would create a lot of pressure; pushing, forcing, fighting, some even laughing, some angrily cursing each other. It was a total shame. This was the noise they had started generating, as they started cursing the priest, trying to leave for their homes. The priest abandoned the Alter and Mass, off his tent, and made for the protection of the church. He and a couple of Liturgy people closed the doors of the church behind them, locked and barred all the doors with the church's benches. Those liturgy people who were at the gates, when they realized what was happening, abandoned the gates and run for their dear lives, to their homes.

In the resulting melee and stampede, Saverio tried to keep a good grip of Tsitsi's hand, as he makes for the opening, which had been ever expanding, as people broke the gates and the durawall down. In the pushing and forcing; someone strikes Saverio by the eye. He blinks in pain, and let go off Tsitsi's hand. He touches his eye in pain, howling. He lost Tsitsi in this melee. By the time he gets control of his bearing, he tries to look around for her, but he couldn't find her. He hears the painful cries of people ahead, behind, besides him. He feels their pain, in his bearing. He barely is breathing, so heavy with strain and exhaustion. He manages to keep to his feet, as he sometimes jumps, stampedes on those who had fallen, on the ground now full of water. The rain hasn't stopped, so he can barely see his way, or who he is stamping with his feet.

Eventually, when he gets through the gates, he is so overcome with the pressure and strain that he faints, as he hits and bowls over the other side of Throgg Morton Avenue.

When he wakes up, he could still hear the whining and whimpering of people and the ambulance vehicles, as they cart people off to Harare general hospital. In the ambulance vehicle he is in, he tries to check around him for Tsitsi, but couldn't find her. He doesn't know who to ask, for he doesn't know anyone who would know her in this vehicle. He could see a lot were dealing with an assortment of injuries, some were passed out. Some more were still being loaded into this ambulance.

He raises himself from his ambulance bed, straightens himself up, and he feels a sickly nauseous feeling, trying to overpower him.

He grips the bars in the ambulance to steady himself. He stretches, steadies himself as he walks out of the ambulance. The ambulance paramedics try to stop him, but he just brushes them aside. He walks slowly back into the church. It seems like a cataclysmic scene, the scene he is confronting. There are now a few family people crying, huddling around four corpses. The priest is on his Alter, alone, praying for these people, still telling them they were going to hell.

"It's a great loss. I pray that you take the spirits of the dead four into your kingdom, father. I know they died because they were sinners. Forgive them, oh, lord. I love you, oh, lord. Give them peace now…"

The priest is droning on and on, without anyone listening to him. He is in his throne, in his heaven. All the other people were in hell. It is still raining, a light taping cold rain. Saverio knows he has to check who the four were. So, he gathers courage as he breaks through the circle of the relatives, open the first corpse, to discover she is an old lady he couldn't recognize. The second corpse is that of the whoring choir conductor. The third one is of the young thieving treasurer, and then he comes to the forth one. He opens the plastic blanket. She is smiling starkly up to him, in hell.

Saverio faints again.

I AM NOW BULLET-PROOF

Celine was her name; nineteen ninety one was the year. She was my first cut into the treacle world of relationships. We were doing our "O" levels at Nyatate secondary school. We were madly in love. At least, that's what we thought. As proof, I offer, tongue in cheek, this evidence: I walked with her every day from school. And I argue this evidence's validity thus: spending those few brief moments of time in between places our parents require us to be is the quintessential defining of commitment for young lovers.

My adoration for her was a map to a new world. She was small, fragile, and light in complexion. She was truthful, genuine, faithful, and loving. To this day, my heart and mouth has always been filled with praise for her. And, praise is a language that is too difficult to separate from love. So, I don't; I twist the two together. I knot them together into a braid that might hold more weight to hang the good memories from, rather than the sad moments of my misguided temper.

At that moment in my life, I was dealing with multiple things: my relationship with Celine, puberty, and school. Despite my feelings toward Celine, I was still too young to really understand what I was doing. I just knew that I liked being with her. And, it was a feeling which fed my hormones a heady cocktail, causing me to do crazy things, make poor decisions.

I was also dealing with dissatisfying grades at school. I used to be a top student in my class, but not anymore. I had barely made average grades for each subject. My parents were not happy with my results. This created some turbulence at home, the kind of thing one expects during the teenage years. They thought they knew the reason for my slide into academic mediocrity. So sure of their hypothesis they were that they sat me down and explained to me that my poor performance stemmed from, in their words, "my stupid relationship with Celine."

I didn't agree with them. Parents always look around and blame the newest thing to come along when any change is detected in the behavior of a child. The truth was far more mundane. I had been too playful that term and didn't concentrate on my studies. My parents did not know that I had been playing at school. Worried in an understandable and yet so cliché way, they told me, if I fail my "O" levels, then I will amount to nothing in life, that I should first concentrate on my studies, and that things with Celine will never amount to anything.

Something must have happened to Celine over the months while we were in a relationship. She was evolving, though these things didn't make sense to my young teenage hormone-riddled self. Her behavior was strange. Sometimes, she wanted me to be gentle. Other times, she wanted me to be tough. From moment to moment, I didn't know how to be. Maybe this is how it always is with young love. Celine tried to transmute me even to a molecular level.

But, there was a voice inside of me that knew that something was wrong. Something was telling me that it was time for me to move on and honor my parent's wishes. It must have been a sensation, something that had crossed the river of life with me. This voice, with its message was so clear, must have emanated from the supernatural connection each of us have from the land across the river, the land where time means nothing, where each of us come into being. It was a soundless voice, a tingling feeling, a breath from another dimension. I still perceive it from time to time and contend that this experience, the presence of this breath, this voice, is universal among humanity. In its presence, I always feel, as I am sure all who read that understand do, as if I am exploring an old stream with a new boat.

So, I acted. I broke up with her in the beginning of our second term. She couldn't understand a thing about it. I didn't even have a good reason. I wasn't about to explain to her that a tingling preconscious voice told me to do it. And, I couldn't tell her that my parents felt that having a relationship with her was affecting my performances at school. Both, I knew sounded like lame excuses. Instead, I told her that I just wanted a break. At the time, it sounded like the most palatable reason. Now, I'm not so sure.

Breaking up was very painful for her. For some time, she refused to say hello to me or even to acknowledge my existence. She avoided me at every cause. I knew I had hurt her, but didn't know what to do about it. I concentrated on my study, instead. On my midterm exam, I was able to pull my grade up drastically. My parents were pleased with the result.

Did I feel dissatisfied with her? Did I feel undeserved of her love? Did it have anything to do with something else, something unfathomable yet instrumental in making me feel the way that I did? Could I have said anything to pacify myself of the blame? What can I do to undo the wrong that I might have done to her? Can I go all the way back and correct that wrong? Every relationship is like a window, framed and contained, with a fixed view. One can look in through the window or out through the window. Both perspectives offer a world of perspective.

Once a relationship is over, I like to look in through that relationship as well as out through that same relationship. Waiting for a quiet moment when I can afford the attention to take a glance, there's always an opportunity to develop, to learn something important hiding in the dynamics. This must be one of the reasons why we, as humans, so often think of love as a defining experience of our brief moment in this life.

On my next vacation, I did take a moment to take a reflective walk and ruminate on my moment with Celine. There was still something there which I needed to explore and she was the one I needed to explore it with. Still present and palpable, my adoration for her was, after all, my first map of the new world of adult love. Even though it seemed like it was a lot too late and a lot of things had changed, I went back to the relationship months later, months after I had unilaterally disbanded it in such a shallow manner.

On a Friday afternoon in early September, a month before our final "O" level exam, I was walking with Celine on our way home from school. I had left my books at school because I wanted to return back on Saturday to study at school. There were three roads all through our village, Mapfurira, which is to the north of Nyatate School. We could have taken the one she wanted; the one that goes through the middle of our village. I refused to take that road, though, because I didn't want to be seen with her by my mother. I also wanted a bit of privacy for I was still inhibited somehow to walk with her through the village.

I told her that I didn't want to be around people, that I wanted to be at the margin of the forest and fields. In my hormone-crazed teenage mind, I admit that I was also probably fantasizing of cuddling with her, touching her. So, though I convinced her to take the road that passes through the fields and small bushes to afford us some little bit of privacy, I felt her reticence all over her body. She clearly didn't want to take this road.

And, though she was acting a bit troubled, I couldn't figure out what was bothering her. My mind couldn't touch the reality which my body already understood. We were barely talking by the time we got to the colorful valley. It was so full of spring roses. As it had rained a couple of times during the past week, we were surrounded by the fresh bloom of tulips with friendly pastel faces waving like happy children in the spring's breeze. With its solid wall of trees protecting it, sheltering it, I knew that I couldn't have painted a more perfect place if I were Monet. This was the perfect place for love; it was a shame that we had become so twisted and couldn't connect to it.

Amidst this gorgeous place as we strolled through it silently, fidgety, we bumped into my friend, Nyasha. Instantly, by the look on his face, I realized that he was waiting for Celine. I understood instantly that this was the reason that Celine hadn't wanted to use this road. This place of love was meant for the two of them, not for me. I sniffed the betrayal and seethed.

And, although the realization of this betrayal hit me like a big wind, I forced myself to calm down a bit. I struggled there to catch my breath as we came upon him, there, waving weakly, obviously trying to dig quickly for some kind of plausible explanation. I don't know why he should have felt stupid, though; I was the one fit to wear that hat. All along, I thought that they were just friends. I had never thought in my wildest imaginations that Nyasha could be interested in Celine. We said 'hello' to him. I asked him pointedly what he was waiting for. Coming up short for a plausible story, he lied lamely and said he was just resting on his way to the shops.

But, this place was on his way home. It was nowhere near the shops. The shops were on the other side of the school.

My blood throbbed. I told him that he could have Celine if he was waiting for her. He denied and refused my offer. Celine was quiet all along. Her face was slicked with sweat. I asked her to stay back with Nyasha if she wanted to. She didn't say anything to me. I was boiling with anger. I knew she wanted to stay with Nyasha, but she decided to leave the scene with me. I was beyond reasoning with her. After we left Nyasha, I started provoking her. She told me that they were not yet dating. Unfortunately, this was not what I was hearing in the spaces between her words. In there, I heard desire.

This irked me. I started calling her despicable names, names I regret and admit here in the hopes for absolution. I used words like whore, bitch, stupid, and two timing brat. She tried to plead with me. But, I was shouting hard at her. My blood was pumping through my ears. All I could hear was the pump of that violent thing in me, that thing that goes crazy when we feel as if we've been wronged. And, so, I responded. I responded in the worst way possible. My mouth spit out the shit that I'd eaten, all of that early teenage crap which we feed ourselves when we fool ourselves into thinking that what we feel is love. And, I was so full of it.

She started crying. Her crying made me feel a bit better. I left her behind while she begged me to come back, telling me that we could work things out. But, I wasn't listening. I kept walking. I returned back to school where I had left my books. In a quiet corner, I tried to read my books until almost dark, but was not grasping anything. I just stared at the words and the lines. In the spaces between, I melted through all of the memories good and bad of my moments with Celine. And, at the end as I packed up, I found resolve. This was the last time I returned back to a relationship.

Even now, I am now trying to listen to these words to find the wisdom in both the good and bad decisions I've made. These words are the sounds of the stones that I have used to guide my path, the path which I hope will, one day, help me to define my life as a success. One of my best friends openly told me that I don't know what I want in life. Maybe, I don't know what I want in love is a better summation. Is he correct? I could tell this friend of mine that I have learned when to accept the limits of a relationship, and that, thanks to the lessons I've learned through examination after reexamination, I would go beyond the limits of what I was once capable.

He might answer me that my behavior was all part and parcel of my not knowing what I want in life. And, he may be right. Certainly, I am not trying to excuse myself of the wrong that I did to Celine. I am saying, though, that I did what I needed to do for who I was at that point in my life. I don't regret the decisions that I made. I am also saying that now I breathe with the knowledge that the memories, when you hold them in your heart, are always enough to sustain a dream of the future which is so much better than living in the shadows of a past.

Most importantly, I am also saying loudly and clearly a heartfelt, "I am so sorry, Celine."

Recognize this act for what it is: I have challenged myself to become a bigger person. Haven't I managed to open up these memories and enfold them onto this paper? These memories shift into shapes on this piece of paper. It is a fearless act, to put these ugly moments onto paper. And, I recognize a growing strength in who I am and what I believe by doing this. Burn this paper if you like, burn these memories. A hope will always linger that another copy is floating about somewhere, somehow. You see, the voice shaped here has now become bullet proof.

HEARTS ARE VICTORS

Maybe...
Maybe, we might be able to still be friends, though so much of life has happened to both of us.

Maybe, she might even still be unattached even though it's been years since I have seen her. My mind recalled the shudders of a name. I reached; I touched; and I attained some sense just beyond waking and, in that state, beheld a wishing well and in it a returning hope, a glimmering, shimmering hope...my eyes opened to find that I was still there, uncomfortable, in my seat on the airplane still finding my way home again.

Collecting my wits, there, at the end of the dream, I reflected on the five years which were just now drawing to a close during which I had pursued my studies in America. It had not been my intention to go in the first place, but events had rushed me there. In those five years in Florida's Fort Lauderdale County, I had finished my studies and gotten some sort of sane grip on my shattering life. I simply had trusted my body to release the lost things when the time was right. In those five years, I had also learned to let go of painful memories.

As I disembarked from my flight arriving at Harare International Airport, I had on my mind a craving to set my eyes on her once more. By seeing her, perhaps, I could be able to erase her completely out of my life, especially if she changed over the years. Time was bound to have taken its toll on her beauty and figure. Deep down, though, I was lying to myself; that what had held everything together was pursuance of knowledge. It simply was a deeply held attraction for the other and that it was now impulses and actions that were choosing themselves justly.

Could she still be in love with me?

I went through Customs. A few minutes later, I was at the outer terminal where my family was waiting for me. There were my father and mother. I couldn't locate my sister, Lorraine.

She had promised me she will be there, but she wasn't anywhere to be found. After hugging and kissing with my parents, I finally answered my mother's question on how it felt to be back after all those years. As we parked our car in the western parking-lot, there came my sister with someone who seemed stunningly beautiful and compellingly familiar.

I didn't have another chance to look at the girl since I was rushing toward my sister for a hug.

"Dessie!"

That was all my sister could manage to say. I gave her a big hug. It was great to see my sister again. We have always been very close because sister and I were the only children in our family.

Peering closer into my sister's eyes, I just couldn't help it, but said.

"Lorraine, you look stunning. You haven't aged a bit."

"Oh, my amorous brother! He is his usual self, again!"

My sister was already getting into the drift of the conversation. She was enjoying the needling. She always accused me of being a great lover, of always unashamedly piling up superlatives on beauty, of being a romanticist at heart. Since being a romanticist at heart kept one's chances open!

"You know, I mean it. You seem to become more beautiful as you mature." And continued,

"I wonder who the hell is the lucky bugger seeing such a beautiful lady like you."

"Hey, am I supposed to answer that question?"

She was smiling sweetly.

"Yeah, why not, big girl?"

"Well, there is someone."

Dreamily, I thought, Lucky old bugger, some guys have all the luck in the world!

"Would you like to meet him?"

"Of course, I would love to meet my future brother-in-law."

"Ok, this reminds me of something else."

She giggled like a little girl.

"There is someone who came to welcome you home, too."

As she said this, she turned around and stepped aside a little to show me her friend. I almost forgot about my sister's friend in the heat of our welcoming exchanges. I raised my eyes from Lorraine's and rested them on that stranger. My heart stuttered with purple clots of manacled voltage. Sweet, Molly Malone! My world was; my world was not! I looked at her again. Our eyes locked instantly. We held on to our eye contact for God knows how many seconds, minutes, or lives. I don't know. Damn, seeing her caused some familiar feelings to rise within me. The warmth rising within me felt hot, fast, and furious. We were timeless. I knew I had met her before, yet it appeared fresh as if I met her only yesterday.

"Hello Des, welcome home."

She said that in a clipped, matter of fact voice like a queen in the castle for a loss, as if nothing happened between us before to make us warm or cold of the other. I managed to still down the surging hope, the poignant pains, those disturbing memories. My voice suited the occasion so very well.

"Hi, it's good to be back. Thanks for coming, Lisa."

"How was it like in America? I heard you now have a doctorate degree?"

I hesitated to tell her that it was so difficult to cross borders, languages and cultures. It was impossible to overcome those challenges without suffering to a certain degree. One could learn, grow and adapt to a new environment, but never can be the same person after the experience. No one ever returns unscathed. I couldn't share my thoughts with her yet. The time was not yet right.

There was nothing in her voice, no warmth, not even the slightest hint of the love that we had shared. But, what more could I expect from her. It's me who had run away in the first place. It's me who chickened out. Why had I expected more? I thought I had assured myself that she didn't mean anything, anymore.

"It was o.k. out there."

We started talking about my studies because it seemed a much safer topic. Lorraine said that Lisa could offer me a lift back home. I was surprised to hear it because I expected that my sister would take me home.

Lorraine was at her best fixing and facilitating mood. How had she duped Lisa into giving her a lift to welcome me at the airport? I couldn't have said anything about that even though I was thinking it was not fair of me to have to thrust myself upon her as if I deserved her help and time.

Lorraine joined Mother and Father carrying some of my luggage into our parents' car and drove off first. Melissa and I followed in Melissa's silver blue Renault Megane. We cleared town and were in Samora Michael Road on our way to Warren Park where my parents lived. We remained silently engrossed in our own thoughts. It was becoming absurd that we remain silent any longer. I started to talk.

"What have you been up to Lisa?"

"Des, nothing very special, really."

She stopped when the light turned red as she got busy in slowing down and changing into lower gears. When she completely stopped the car, she continued.

"I completed my MBA in finance with UNISA two months ago. I managed to climb a few steps of our workplace's ladder."

"Not workplace's ladders and snakes?"

We couldn't help giggling and the humor here was not happiness itself, but the consequence of happiness.

Picking up on this dangling strand, I wanted to continue the moment. "Are you still at Price Waterhouse?"

"Oh, yeah"

"Then, you must be top brass there. It must be a very special place for you as you have been working there for a long time."

"In a way..." Lisa left off, before continuing, "It is special."

I waited, thinking that she was going to tell me why it was special for her. She offered no explanation, but said, "Why haven't you married yet, Des?"

She smiled mischievously. I was captivated by her openness and originality.

"I have been really busy with my studies. I don't think I was ready yet. How about you?"

"No, of course I am not married!"

She really was smiling at that moment. I didn't realize how stupid of me to ask her that question. After all, she wouldn't want to come to the airport to welcome me. Why hasn't she married? She must be receiving proposals on a daily basis. Why was she still single? What was she waiting for? I had to know.

"How come you are still single?"

"No one will have me."

Seriously?

"Really...?"

She laughed with merry amusement. It seemed like her happiness was coming from her heart. She shrugged, warming to my playful teasing.

"You are lying. I am sure a lot of young men are crazy about you."

"Maybe! But, I have been too busy to think about that. In fact, I didn't feel I should think about marriage, yet."

"You don't like talking about yourself?"

"There is not much to talk about..."

Is there really nothing much to talk about her?

She really didn't have anyone special to talk about. A lot of young men out there must have broken hearts because of her. I was engrossed in this thought-train. Words had settled like dust on our tongues, unspoken, when we turned onto my parent's driveway.

Now, it was her turn.

"You didn't convince me why you are still single yourself. I'm sure there must be a lot of beautiful girls you could have settled for in America."

I wasn't sure anymore why I hadn't settled down with someone. The reasons I used to offer myself didn't appear plausible anymore. They now sounded ridiculous and silly like stray ideas born out of stray words. Before answering her question, our conversation got interrupted by noise outside. As we entered the gates, friends and relatives welcomed me. After finishing her drink, Melissa went back to her place in Eastlea. She promised to come back for the party that night.

She came back at eight in the evening for the party. I tried to have a few undisturbed moments with her. We got interrupted by others. I didn't seek her this time. Instead, I put aside my need to spend alone-time with her. I knew she would heed the call and come for me. I had to mingle with everyone at the party since it was for my homecoming. When it was time for dancing, it seemed obvious that even for that I wasn't going to get an opportunity for that. They were always a lot of people ready to walk me to the dance-floors. This seemed the case on her side too. It meant we were never available at the same time to take the chance to dance together.

At around midnight, people started leaving the party. Dancing finally came to an end. As the guests were leaving, they express their farewells. When all those who wanted to go had gone, someone suggested for a last waltz, a proper end for a wonderful party. This time I didn't wait for fate to pair us.

I asked Melissa for a dance. It was the word that saw the other words into the interior space of my need. She moved into my arms. I knew it was home to be in her arms again. Hunger for her hit me like a punch in the guts. I saw with a stab of fierce male appreciation, the electricity, the heat that was between us. There was a binding irresistible force. She was also aware of the connection, and the oneness that we had always felt for each other. It was still there even after the long separation that had almost destroyed the connection.

This was always where I had wanted to be, right there in her arms, in the deepest intimate place next to her.

We couldn't talk because talking was out of context.

Only to feel! That was what we did. Were they merely hormones that were making her blood race and desire surge in her veins, beating in an insistent song? This was the song that had been an acappella solo for so many years when I was in the USA. Before the song ended, I had maneuvered her to the door.

We went outside for fresh air. We sat on the chairs in the backyard in the flower garden. We didn't talk. Words were lame and swallowed by the wonderful moon in the sky. All we did was to wallow in the yellow flowers of light and melting slivers. We didn't want to mess up this reunion.

The special moment didn't last long because we were called back into the drawing room as our last guests started bidding us farewell. Melissa was ready to leave, as well. I walked her to her car. In the following weeks, with an excuse to consult her on employment prospects, I went to see her at her home and her workplace. Soon after, we were going out.

Meanwhile I got a job as a financial director at a very famous firm in Harare. My life progressed well. Melissa and I remained wary of committing to each other. On the sixth month of my return, I decided to host a thank-you-party to those who had been helpful on my return. It was the end of November. People were already in a partying mood. Everyone I invited came to my party; it was very successful. Early in the morning when everyone had departed, I asked Mellissa to stay for a little while. But, what could I have said? Maybe I could only have raised my hands in praise to all of us who had survived ourselves!

Did I have to tell her of the hurt that I felt when I heard the rumors about her dating someone else, and that she was about to marry him? Did I have to tell her that they had told me that it was love and that I couldn't have believed it was anything otherwise? I couldn't have believed that that relationship was only coffee-in-the-restaurant and friendship, but also sex. I believed it was with love? And love being the worse of all these that I could only have scared away. Did I have to tell her of the crying, the paining, the hurting, and the hopelessness? I chickened out. I ran away. My pride had forced me never to enquire on those rumors about her throughout all the years I was in America. After all, after that lack of trust that I had shown, what right did I have to ask her about us again? Could she have accepted my apologies?

She had erred too. In her stubbornness and pride, she had never asked about me after I left. She had never even tried to contact me to put those rumors to rest. At least, it was common gossip that she was seeing that other guy. How could I wait for her voice in the empty holes of the telephone telling me it was me whom she loved? How could I pine for her virtual call from her soulless cell-phone!

She could have tried to explain. She should have asked me why I had started slackening. I needed assurance. I could have understood if she tried, but she had kept to herself.

But, that morning we made love. We were like two drowning strangers. It was for the first time in five years. After, we pillow-talked everything which had transpired between us, we agreed that we were all at fault for the breakdown of our relationship. We still loved each other. The separation had not changed anything about how we felt about each other. Whatever didn't kill us, only made us stronger. We agreed we could still give it another go. Years of distance and the rumors seemed to fail to destroy what we felt for one another.

At round three in the morning, I knew that Melissa had to go back to her place. Yet, no one seemed to be in a hurry to leave each other's company. On my side, it was this feeling that I had left-off something very important, something that I should have told her, but this time she really meant it when she said, "I really should be going now."

Then, everything came back to me like autumn, an equinoctial eye spying on the departing summer, and the coming winter, on us, too. I became her and she became me like autumn looks at both the summer and the winter. Melissa shaped herself well inside this bubble. Everything became me and her and the morning light around us.

"Stay with me, Melissa, for the rest of the night."

"The night? But, it's already morning, Des."

She left my request unanswered. I rushed in to assure her.

"Not only this night or morning, Lisa. I mean forever."

She was silent, undecided. Was she suffering from champagne jitters? I mused to myself. That feeling you have when you are about to open a bottle of champagne, just before you pop the cork, you get nervous because you don't know if it's going to go *kaboom* in your face or just ease off with a nice, soft and easy fizz.

I rushed in again.

"Melissa, we have been so stupid to allow our pride to wreck us. I don't want it to affect us again. I don't want any more misunderstanding between us. I want us to be together forever, babe. I want to wake up beside you all the coming mornings. Please don't leave me now. I would never be able to live without you again, babe."

This time, I waited for her reply. She remained silent as if she felt doubtful. She raised her eyes and looked directly into mine. I saw simmering tears in her misty light brown eyes. With tears of happiness, she smiled sweetly, contentedly. She floated into my arms. Somewhere, in my heart, curtains lifted up. The sun was shining brightly again enveloping me in the morning's true and innocent light. Yet?

"Please Melissa..."

"Sshii, sshii..."

She shook her head and blocked my mouth from saying anything more with her spread fingers as she caressed me playfully and sharpened my sighted mind with these incandescent graphics finger-drawn on my lips. The echoes of our interlocking rhythms pulsed throughout the room; then, she kissed me full on the lips and said, "Yes...forever..."

161

This time, she kissed me provokingly. It seemed nothing else mattered. What else could have really mattered now other than kissing this beautiful woman? We shared our affection and passion again through our bodies.

I breathed her in, held her in my two hands, and pressed her face onto mine. A thought formed, the sun must really be up in the morning sky for where else could such light be coming from?

MAKEBHA

She was a beautiful girl, light complexioned girl, sweet and very young, only 13 when she was paid lobola for by Obadiah of Hogo Village Seven. Her name was Makebha Kanyawa of Chibvuri Village. When she got married to Obadiah they had stayed with Obadiah' family, his widowed mother, Mai Nyachuru. For the first few years they were happy, shared the same kitchen as woman of this household and Obadiah was so happy, only that Makebha failed to conceive. This caused the couple to start drifting, and a few years later, Obadiah took another wife.

You have done well, my son. I need a grandson and this Ngomwa (Barren woman) of yours isn't going to make it happen.

Mai Nyachuru thanked her son when he brought the new wife home. As per their church's tradition it was allowed for a man to have a concubine of wives, so Makebha accepted this new bride of his husband into the family. She had since moved to her own new home nearby her in-laws, so this new wife joins Makebha in her new home. And this new wife, in the first year of her marriage got pregnant and gave Obadiah his first son. Everyone was happy and Obadiah started ignoring Makebha, started abusing her, would ask her to wait for and work for this new wife, and hardly had time with her in the bedroom.

Where Makebha came from, her family was not of the same faith with Obadiah's family. Obadiah and his family were of the Marange Apostolic Faith and Makebha's family were of the Anglican Faith, so Obadiah and his family connived together to make life such a hellhole for Makebha so that Makebha would give up on the marriage and leave for her family whom they viewed as pagans and were going to Gehenna.

But Makebha loved her husband so she stayed and faced everything doggedly. Obadiah took another wife and could hardly come over to Makebha's bedroom. In the tenth year of their marriage, when Makebha was now even contemplating leaving for her home, she got pregnant.

Instantly Obadiah and his family disputed and disclaimed paternity to the child. Even though everyone told them Makebha was a pious wife, even though Obadiah knew he had slept with Makebha, he refused to accept the child as his, but she also refused to go, telling Obadiah,

This is your child. You know you are the only one I have ever slept with.

I have slept with you all these ten years and you never conceived. You are barren. I can't be the owner of that bastard. You have to leave for your family home. I am not going to take you back to your family, I don't owe your family an explanation, and rather they should apologize for marrying me to you a whore and Ngomwa. I am not going to be responsible for this child of the wilderness.

But this child is your, Obadiah. Makebha insisted, I am not going anywhere. You are the father of my child. You should be happy God has found favour with us, Obadiah.

You mean, God has found favour with you Makebha. Obadiah hit back,

I already have five sons and six daughters from my real wives, as you can see, Ngomwa.

This is your child, Obadiah. I am not going anywhere. I will die here.

I don't care. You were barren all these years. You wasted my time and made people laugh at me. Now some other man who had spiked you not to conceive has impregnated you and you are pilling more shame on me. You think there is anyone out there who believes this is my child, do you. People are laughing at me now, saying I gave you a go ahead to find a donor husband. You have to leave my home now.

But Makebha refused to leave. Obadiah would beat up Makebha. He would take away Makebha's food and throw it in the toilet, would terrorize her, insult her and attempted to kill her several times but always stopped short of it, afraid of the consequences.

But in the 9th month of the pregnancy Obadiah decided the only way to deal with a stubborn Makebha was to beat her on the stomach until she had lost the baby, so he beat Makebha with a strong branch of a tree, until Makebha lost consciousness. The baby she was carrying died in her stomach. A day later she died in labor trying to eject the broken pieces.

Obadiah's family knowing they were going to pay dearly and Obadiah will be arrested or killed by Makebha's brothers decided not to inform Makebha's family of her death and buried her without their knowledge. But the wind whispers are heard far away, so Makebha's family heard of this and didn't waste time reporting this to the police. They stayed put. They knew well what to do.

*****

Kiro na Makebha vakaenda Jorodhani kumusha kuna baba, Who could be singing that song, imitating that prostitute wife of mine thought Obadiah with trepidation. He had started hearing of the stories of Makebha coming from the dead 7 days after they had buried her. It was his neighbor who had told him, but he dismissed it. His neighbor was known to blow midwives tales into proportion. How could people pass around stupid gossips of Makebha coming back alive just to terrorize him? It's only in the bible where stories of Elijah, Moses, Jesus coming back alive when dead could be found. Makebha wasn't these, she was just a prostitute that got what she deserved. He suspected his neighbor of impregnating this prostitute of a wife he had done in. She is bloody rotting in her grave now. These are the thoughts and questions that Obadiah assaulted himself with as he went to sleep with his newest wife, the 5th one.

He didn't tell any of his wives of what he had heard. There was no need to scare them with this story. It was simply a lie!

How could someone who should have hit mid decay status come back, a week after burial alive. This was his last thought as he put out the light and joined the wife on the bed, a traditional mat, with used old blankets and held his wife in his arms

Kiro na Makebha vakaenda Jorodhani kumusha kuna baba. His new wife he is holding in his arms starts a song.

Kana neniwo ndichaenda Jorodhani kumusha kuna baba, Obadiah chorused to the song in his sleep. He is dancing on a fire, a beautiful fire that burns beautifully in his veins as he sings this song with his wife. They were making love and as he hit orgasm he collapsed into a deep trance, and had started hearing Makebha singing the song outside, and he had to call back in chorus. He is deep in a trance so he can't even connect this song to the rumors he had heard. He sang with fervor. He enters a spiritual dimension as he danced on top of the fire without getting burned. He hums, crones to the song the apostolic way. He saw the fire leaping into huge rays around him. He started being airlifted in a ball of fire like

Elijah into the heavens. His wife stayed there below, but her voice could still be heard as he went,

Kiro na Makebha vakaenda Jorodhani kumusha kuna baba.

And he still replied up there, faintly.

Kana Neniwo ndirikuenda Jorodhani kumusha kuna baba.

He kept going up and up, and he didn't feel like alighting off the ball of fire, and then the voice thinned out as he hit the cool clouds and water, things fizzled down, cooled, the fire dies and he is waking from the dream.

He looks around him. It's already morning, the skies are blue, the sun bursting out of Nyanga mountain. The morning birds exploding in tongues of a song of the sun, and he is on his reed mat, but beside the recently deceased Makebha's grave. All around him the graves nod at him in silent complicity with Makebha. He is shook with a fear he can't even fathom. He realizes he was carried to this grave by Makebha in that dream he had. He realizes he was making love to Makebha, as he is fully naked. He runs of the grave, naked. He arrives home as everyone at home was busy trying to figure out what had happened to him, with some of his children already gone to report the missing person report at the chairman's home. The whole household is disturbed beyond belief when they hear of their father's story. The village head and the villagers tell him to right the wrong he did by paying Makebha's family, but Obadiah refuses, saying his faith does not allow him to do that.

*****

Kiro na Makebha vakaenda Jorodhani kumusha kuna baba.

Who is singing, who are you? Where are you Makebha? Obadiah's mother asks as she searches around her to see who was singing that song. She knew who was singing it, it was common knowledge that Makebha was coming back, after she had terrorized Obadiah a couple of days before. Obadiah's mother was scared shit. She didn't know what Makebha will do to her. She wasn't seeing her, and it was broad daylight, only the voice that seemed to be everywhere, steaming her with its hot anger.

She grabs hard the 20 litre tin of water she was carrying on her head, afraid of spilling it with trepidation and fear.

Ndiwe wakandirambanisa nemwana wako, nhasi unochiona. Makebha accuses Obadiah's mother for driving a wedge between her and Obadiah.

No no, it's not me. It's you who was barren. It's you who lost your husband...

Before she could finish, she was whacked on the face, it seemed by a giant hand, as she bellowed,

Yowee...maiwe kani!

She falls on the ground and faints, the can of water spilling on top of her, wetting her back to consciousness in that breathe of a moment. She knew she was in grave danger from the angry monster Makebha. She heaves up in a hurry and hit the cheeks of the land for home, sprinting across Tendanayi bridge where she was coming from Chitsoko gardens where she had been watering her garden patch, and fetching water to use at home. Yet as she belt away she keeps hearing the voice after her.

Kiro na Makebha vakaenda Jorodhani kumusha kuna baba. As a boot hits her by the buttocks and she tumbles in a summersault, collapsing in a ditch off the small walkways to her home. She bellows in plea,

Yowee, sorry muroora Makebha, have mercy!

Mercy, what mercy. Did you have mercy for me as your son terrorized me and killed me? You are the one who supported him. You called me Ngomwa and when God looked upon me with

168

mercy and gave me a daughter you called me a whore. You rejected me. Now you want mercy from me. Today is you end.

Yes, I am so sorry muroora. I did you wrong. I am sorry, have mercy on me. I was a difficult old painful mother-in-law to you, but I never thought my son will kill you. All I wanted was for my son to have a family.

As more and more people come to see the spectacle, including Obadiah, Makebha kept kicking her in-law. No matter how much some people tried to plead on her behalf she was deaf to all these people.

I don't care old witch, today you are going to join me *kwamupfiganebwe*. Let this be the warning to your son to pay my family for the wrong he did to me. Otherwise I won't lay to rest until my family gets recompense!

She shouted out aloud that everyone who was there including Obadiah heard it. But, she kept kicking her in-law like a ball as Obadiah's mother groaned for the last time and drifted with Makebha to the beyond!

TEARS RUN DRY: SUNRISE

The morning following the serious talk with Tatenda, Monica took the earliest bus to Chitungwiza. She wanted to know what was happening to her. The previous night, she hadn't slept well and had a chilling and horrible dream.

In her dream, she saw a form she recognized as Tatenda's chasing her, and that form smacked of something gone awfully wrong. The form was talking of the many people it had wed. It was pursuing her, saying that the time had come for its long awaited wedding with Monica. In fleeing away from that form, she came to an eerie silent place which was infested with many skeletons talking around a fire. The ghostlike form of Tatenda also appeared there.

Encircling her, the skeletons started ululating in congratulatory voices as if the wedding was really happening. The grotesque figures were also dancing with upraised hands, reveling in a song which had words she never had heard before. Some of the skeletons were clapping their bony hands, and whistling joyously. With Monica between them, they started on a silent journey through a very silent cold wasteland, a land so calm, so desolate, a dead land the kind of which she had never seen and never thought existed.

After what appeared an epoch of walking, the skeleton leader of the march announced that they had arrived at their destination and would be meeting with other friends long since departed.

Monica tried to focus her eyes on the place.

It was a dark yawning abyss. She was being drawn compellingly into it. Feeling its pull, she started shrieking, begging to be released.

Yet, she couldn't stop herself being drawn into it. The land's desolation gave her nothing to hold onto, nothing to slow her descent into the yawning darkness. In the dream, everyone had left her, alone and anxious, holding onto some tiny part of her waking consciousness waiting anxiously for the coming sun to bestow light to the hidden parts of her life and chase this darkness away.

Later, she couldn't remember whether she was still dreaming, but the shadows started dimming and disappearing. As she waited, it grew lighter and lighter. The appearance, in the East, of the Morning Star inspired her.

Was she really mistaken?

Was the dream really over?

As Monica arrived at Tatenda's family home, she was surprised to see a lot of people gathered there. Many of them were weeping.

What's the cause of all this sadness? She asked herself.

Then, that feeling of something having gone wrong took root in her. She knew she must find what it was that had taken root? So, she entered the gate and walked straight into the kitchen. Tatenda's mother was crying as well. When she saw Monica, she wept all the more.

Monica knew what was wrong all along. The truth of it was there, in her mind and heart, but somehow she had managed to disdain its voice.

"Tatenda is dead."

"Tatenda is dead."

"Tatenda is dead."

She fainted and was taken to South Medical Hospital in Zengeza.

Meanwhile, the funeral entered its second day amid a lot more tears. People were surprised why a young healthy man had killed himself. Some people concocted a story of an affair that had gone sour. Some people whispered about an evil spirit that rooms in the family house. Some even said that the mother might be the next in line if nothing is done to appease the spirit.

The memory of a horrendous car wreck surfaced. The community remembered that Tatenda's step father and his brothers, a step brother and a half brother, all died while Tatenda was still in his teens. They remembered that his grandmother had died too, a couple of years before. Clearly, a shadow hung over this family. Worse, they wondered if they, perhaps, had been jinxed as well.

Some even guessed that the young man may have had an incurable disease, but little did they know how very close to the truth they were. The truth remained known only to Tatenda's mother who revealed nothing. She didn't want to bring shame to her son's name and certainly not to the family's reputation.

With grief, sorrow and sadness, Tatenda was buried in the afternoon. Later on, the same day, Monica gained consciousness. She was surprised to find herself in the hospital. When she asked the nurse why she was there, she was told she had fainted at a funeral. Then, she remembered everything and begged the nurse to let her out of the hospital. She hoped to still see him. Little did she know: he had already been given back to the Earth.

The hospital refused to release her because she wasn't yet strong enough. The next afternoon, Tatenda's mother came to the hospital to see how she was faring. Needing her closeness and to share with her the truth, Tatenda's mother brought her home with her.

When they arrived home, they went to the cemetery together in order for Monica to say her last goodbyes, though belatedly, to her love. She cried and cried; for Monica, it was an absurd and shocking loss. She still knew nothing beyond that last mysterious confusing moment she had shared with Tatenda. Tatenda's mother held her in her arms, and after some time, encouraged her to spare herself since she could end up ill if she kept grieving.

What could be the meaning of the conversation she had with Tatenda before his death? He had talked of everything being out of his grasp, maybe death was, but how could he have known he was going to die. After all, he had killed himself and why? Why suicide? Behind these questions, Monica knew there was an explanation for everything that happened, and she really wanted to know what it was. After a terrible night of torture, trying to envisage the reason behind the suicide, she decided to ask Tatenda's mother what had made him kill himself. Luckily, she found her alone in her bedroom and willing to tell everything that transpired.

Tatenda's mother told her about the HIV Tatenda had contracted from a previous relationship. Monica instantly recognized that his guilt was the cause of suicide. So I have the disease as well? But why didn't he tell me about this? What was he so afraid of? Did he think I would hate him and kill myself if I knew? Am I going to die, am I, really...? Am I really going to die?

Monica asked herself these questions as Tatenda's mother spoke to her. Reading her mind, Tatenda's mother said, "He didn't tell you everything because it was very shameful for him. He killed himself because he blamed himself for the wrong that he had done to you. He found himself undeserving of life. I hope you will look at the situation differently. I hope you will have courage enough to look at your situation in a positive way. Even if you have the virus, you still have many years to live. You could still enjoy your life and could love again, even though it may be very difficult to forget what Tatenda did to you."

Surprisingly, Monica said, "I now understand why he didn't want me to know; it's because he wanted to protect me, he thought

I could kill myself if I became aware of my condition? I know he was faithful to me, and what happened before he met me, was a mistake. He shouldn't have killed himself."

"Yes, but he also viewed that as his own mistake and that his mistake endangered you, too. He felt so bad, so undeserving to live; that's why he killed himself."

"I don't even know where to begin." Monica wondered. "And I don't even know how I feel about everything, I just don't know...but I don't have any intentions of killing myself for it's against my belief. At least for his sake and mine, I will not kill myself and, from now on, I will try to live positively and hopefully."

Quite happily, Tatenda's mother agreed with her, "That's great! How about if we start by making sure what your condition really is; you may not even have the virus at all! I will accompany you to your doctor if you want me to."

"When?"

"It's all up to you, I should think."

"How about now?"

"You are unbelievably courageous, child."

"I don't feel like delaying it for another moment."

"Let's go then."

Tatenda's mother encouraged her as she started walking towards the door. On the way to the door, she said, "I am happy you haven't lost hope; you know what: it's the most important thing, child. Don't be afraid because I will always be there for you. Whenever you need me, you can call upon me, daughter."

"Thank you. I will remember that, Mom." She gratefully accepted.

They went to her doctor together where blood samples were taken. Then, they returned to their homes to wait for the results.

Three times during the week, Tatenda's mother came to visit her and, on one of the days, she took her to a counseling agency. Monica joined a group of people who had been diagnosed with the virus. She found out that they, once every week, met for lectures on living positively with the virus. Also, they organized sporting activities, voluntary work, and public lectures on the disease.

By the end of the week, she wasn't afraid of facing the results because, even if the results were to come back positive, she realized she still had a life to live and how best to live it. When the appointment day arrived she went to see her doctor who confirmed her worse suspicion. Yes, the dreaded virus had taken root inside of her. After an important medical and good health habits talk from the doctor, she found Tatenda's mother and a friend she had met at the group meetings waiting for her in the doctor's waiting room.

Monica didn't have to tell them; they understood. Tatenda's mother enfolded her in her arms. With the young man at her left side and Tatenda's mother at her right, their hands entwined together, they assured one another that they will always be together, come what may. They left the doctor's office for home committed to no longer shed tears.

It was time to let the tears run dry.

Printed in the United States
By Bookmasters